FIVE DAYS OF BLEEDING

FIVE DAYS OF BLEEDING

a novel by
Ricardo Cortez Cruz

BLACK ICE BOOKS

NORMAL

Published by FC2 with support given by the English Department Unit for Contemporary Literature, and the Illinois Arts Council

Address all inquiries to: FC2, Unit for Contemporary Literature, Campus Box 4241, Illinois State University, Normal, IL 61790-4241

Five Days Of Bleeding
Ricardo Cortez Cruz

ISBN: Paper, 1-57366-003-5

Produced and printed in the United States of America

ACKNOWLEDGMENTS

Actually, these are more like liner notes:

First, I would like to thank Curtis White for his continued encouragement and friendship while guiding me as a mentor. I praise writers Larry McCaffery, Sterling D. Plumpp, Robert Elliot Fox, Mark Amerika, Darius James, Robert Coover, Raymond Federman, Charles Johnson, Reggie Osse of *The Source*, Eugene B. Redmond, Dennis Brutus, and bell hooks for their special support. A word of gratitude to Clarence Major, Charles H. and N. Mildred Nilon, and Fiction Collective Two for the "tour de force" debut novel *Straight Outta Compton*. I wish continued success to *The Kenyon Review*, *Fiction International*, *Postmodern Culture*, and *The Illinois Review*, where excerpts of *Five Days of Bleeding* have appeared in slightly different form. Also, I gotta give props to *Black Ice*, Alexander Laurence and *Cups*, Doug Rice and *Nobodaddies*, and Southern Illinois University-Carbondale for letting me show my stuff. Zu-Zu Girl's last line in this novel and "I got the blues of a fallen teardrop" were used from Sterling D. Plumpp's magnificent book *Blues: The Story Always Untold* with the author's kind permission.

Special thanks to Clarence Major (you a badd boy when you slang that writing-thing).

Shouts out to Charles and Victoria Harris, Kent Haruf, Beth Lordan, Ron Sukenick, Robert Sutherland, Richard "Pete" Peterson, Ron Strickland, Ken Seib, and Steve Herald. And to the home slices (black men united): my brother, Derrick A. Milling-EL; cousins Tony Cruz and Michael Simpson for their generous support of *Compton* and neverending friendship; best men Greg Tyus and Rodney B. Cruz for their love (I know you got my back); cousin and civil rights law-man Garth Minor for cracking me up when I needed the laugh (represent me, man); and, Terry L. Hardin from around-the-way for the strong art/work.

I can't stop until I recognize some major voices: sister and brother, Malisa Angela Cruz and Theodore Quintota Cruz (Missy and Quiny, cain't nobody take away our heart); Rev. Tyus, Esther Tyus, and Candy Tyus—my dad, mom, and sister away from home; my family in South Carolina (Rev. Willie C. and Irene Milling) and Brooklyn, New York (Willie C., Jr., and family); and, most important after my beautiful wife, my parents Theodore and Carol Cruz, whose brilliant wisdom I remember in everything I do.

To all yaw, peace.

FOR
        MY
BELOVED CAROL

                    I am a song-Bird
                                like John Coltrane
                        saying
                "My One and Only Love"

to you
over and over again…

In the beginning was the beat, and the beat was the rhythm of God, and the rhythm of God became the harmony of humanity, and where there is harmony there is peace.

—Clarence Glover, in "Spirituality: An African View," *Essence*, December 1987

FREE DANCE IN CENTRAL PARK

Planet Rock

"I'm the DJ, he's the rapper," Chops said, pointing his big finger in my face as if the planet had just begun to spin.

It was night, and the white clouds laughed at Chops until their stomachs burst and they cried. Linton Johnson, a Rastafarian-feeling Black nigger with mustard seed, scronched down in front of our faces and yelled out that New York's Central Park was Nigger heaven.

"Holdup. Wait a minute.

"Is Nigger heaven a Carl Van Vechten novel or a cabin in the sky or a Black place or a sanctuary where August hams grow wild or a haven for blues or what?" I asked.

Johnson blew happy dust in my face. "Bottle it," he said.

Along with Johnson, a slew of negroes knocked boots in the park and celebrated in the dust like it was nothing. A Black Monday. At the party, the stock market came crashing, niggers playing the numbers and looking as if they were straight proud to be living in the hustle of Harlem. Like crows, they picked their favorite numbers and scratched them down on their palms, some of them singing "Downtown" and "I'm in Love" by Lillo Thomas, a homeboy who sung for Hush Productions.

Meantime on somebody's color television: "The problem is, when these films like New Jack City play there are so few of them until blacks flood the theatres and make a major event out of them."

On BET, "If it's on the screen, we're definitely on the scene."

On MTV, "Let love rule."

On USA Up All Night, "Don't go away. Stay right here to watch more horror-madness."

Whites nervously peeked out of their windows and saw dinge and charcoal everywhere, dope as art, Guns N' Roses taking over their houses sky-high above the Harlem juke-joints north of the park.

One Nation Under A Groove

Chops' joke that I do all the talking was very funny, but Johnson was seriously looking for more entertainment to show off in the park, protest the absence of social change, his forehead roughed up like the pavement of a bad road.

"The race problem in the United States has resolved itself into a question of saving black men's bodies and white men's souls," Johnson said.

Under the moon, I passed for white. "Are you Lyndon Johnson or James Weldon Johnson or Johnson & Johnson from *Jet* and *Ebony* or baby powder?" I asked.

Mr. Johnson—calm, slender, as immaculate as Madonna singing "I'm waiting for you to justify my love," stood on the narrow strip of wooden stage between the footlights set up in the park and the green grass.

"The name is Linton. If you can't say or play it, then take yourself, that sad girl with you, and the fat Sloppy Joe and go home."

Chops started feeling self-conscious, trying to tuck his shirt in.

"Who made you head negro, Lint-head?" I asked, covering for Chops.

11

Johnson ran up and pushed us into the grass, then laughed. "That stuff was cold, wasn't it?" he asked, the earth making me soiled.

"Yeah, baby," I answered. "Yeah." I blew him off.

Birth of the Cool

Chops and Zu-Zu Girl started cutting up, tripping and rolling over sharp blades of wet brown grass they had found in patches near a wooden park bench. Zu-Zu was singing the blues. We got up and sent Johnson off with a smile that we inverted once his back was turned. Then we sat down on the bench, our booties itching for a 12-inch scratch. My cheeks scooted along the hard wood. "Wiggle it, just a little bit, baby," the bench said.

Zu-Zu laughed, like the bench was a black man talking to her. Chops laid out.

"You got it good and that ain't bad," said Zu-Zu.

"Murdah in the first degree," I told Zu-Zu.

"You can't keep a good man down," said Zu-Zu.

Chops was laid back, doing statues of liberty with his fingers. "Lucy's in the sky with diamonds," said Chops, downing a Third Stream from his bottle. He was a chaser of the American Dream.

Zu-Zu snatched the pastries out of Chops' other hand and went off. "Straighten up and fly right," said Zu-Zu. "Your jelly roll is good."

The pigeons picked crumbs out of Zu-Zu's palm. Chops offered Zu-Zu his bottle.

"Excuse me," said Chops, "but would you like a heavy-wet, cherry bounce, gooseberry wine, fine, cold-without, Tom-and Jerry or mountain dew?"

Zu-Zu whipped Chops with a coke stare and flicked her remaining crumbs into the trash can. From her tube top, she produced half of a club sandwich and stuck it in her mouth.

"I'd like a John Collins or blue ruin or apple-jack or black velvet or twopenny or white-ale or dog's nose or whisky toddy or London particular," said Zu-Zu.

Zu-Zu sung the "Laughing Song," then broke out smiling, her big mouth full of government cheese. She leaned over and smacked Chops in the face, her dark nipples giving a mean look, hating her for wearing a white boob-tube.

Chops pointed at her small blackened nipples and began singing "Penny Lover, just walk on by" like he was Lionel Richie.

Zu-Zu raised her black fist, and for a second Chops thought of Angela Davis and those terrible afros. He reeled, then tried to get himself together.

I grabbed Zu-Zu's punch and told her to stop. "Excuse me, pardon me, don't let me get in your way," I told Zu-Zu, "but this ain't Queens or Manhattan or Long Island or Greenwich or Harlem. This downtown. You just can't go around smacking everybody in the face. Dig?"

Zu-Zu sung "Dead Drunk Blues," booze trickling out of her mouth. She tugged on the ruffles of her top so it wouldn't slip any further down.

Mercy, Mercy, Mercy

"You sho' is big, Zu-Zu," said Chops. Chops was about to fly away over a bird chest. Meantime, I wondered what she was doing without a strapless bra and whether or not she had always been stuffing her top with sandwiches or Manwiches that were meals.

"Shaka Zulu," I said. I didn't know what else to say.

Zu-Zu moved over and smacked Chops in the mouth like a woman warrior. "Bop," she said, her boob-tube shaking a teeny tiny bit as she danced in the park.

"I wish I could shimmy like my sister Kate," said Zu-Zu.

"Party people!" I shouted. "Party people!"

Chops looked at me like I was fickle. "Let the whole world know," he said, sarcastically. "Do it 'til you're satisfied."

I'm Shoutin Again

I'm dancin' on the benches while Chops sits and stares, his mouth open, his eyes on Zu-Zu's chest. He thinks about Zu-Zu's skin resembling burned-out volcanic ash and her breasts slowly changing into black marble. I shout some more.

"Get up, get into it, get involved!" I yell. It's as if I'm shouting at the breasts.

Zu-Zu breaks down and does a war dance downtown, pulling her boob-tube up and down again, lots of black folks gathering around her and jeering.

Chops grips my shoulder, a small amount of grass appearing in his other hand. "You got to tell them," he says. "Soylent green is people."

"Chops, are there no cheap magician tricks or pestilence that you won't stoop to?" I grab Zu-Zu around her waist, and we do it to a little east coast swing.

"You can swing it, too," said Chops.

Zu-Zu laughs and smooches with me while we slowly spin in the soft, thick mud. "My Man-Of-War," sings Zu-Zu, like we're in the trenches. Then she sings "That Thing Called Love."

Rum and Coca-Cola

Zu-Zu was a mighty tight woman, moaning blues, caffeine and alcohol keeping her going.

"Swing low, chariot," Zu-Zu whispered. Zu-Zu was ready to go. She sung "New York Tombs."

Chops, now collecting pennies in an empty 40-ounce bottle of Old E, came over and whispered in my ears. "What's wrong with Zu-Zu?" he asked.

Zu-Zu was off into her own world, everybody drinking moonshine but her.

"What did I do to be so black and blue?" asked Zu-Zu. She threw her bottle away like it was water.

"Take it easy, Zu-Zu," I said. I dropped my bottle of coke and gave her a warm-fuzzy.

Zu-Zu pulled back, then reeled her self back in. "Don't hug me," she said. She was as timid and tender as the still of the night, dark bruises rearing their ugly heads on the blackest parts of her.

What Is There To Say?

Zu-Zu peeled my fingers off her skin and turned away. She sang "In A Silent Way."

"She's been sleeping with the enemy," said Chops. "She's got it bad and that ain't good."

"That nigga is just gonna drag you down, Zu-Zu," I said.

Chops reached into his pocket and dug out a chunk of government cheese. "Want a piece?"

Looking helpless, Zu-Zu shrugged her shoulders. "I need love in the worst sort of way," she said. She took off her skirt and raised her tube top to her head, even startling the old, tired relaxer in her hair.

Chops unzipped his pants, pushed Zu-Zu down on the bench and hit her on the side of the face, smearing her rouge into blood.

Then like he had seen on an erotic voodoo film showing on a residence's nighttime television, Chops jumped her bones.

"Stop!" I yelled. I was afraid for Zu-Zu. Chops had white man's disease. He could barely jump, his stomach so full of fat that niggas passed by and called him an all-natural big

15

greasy potato chip with no preservatives.

Squirming to get comfortable on two boards, Zu-Zu looked like the heroine of a silent movie laid down on some railroad track waiting for the train or a hero to come. Chops leaped back-and-forth over her throat, his curly fro too scared stiff to move.

Zu-Zu blew her cool. "I hate a man like you," she said. "Are you going to jump my bones all night or take off your pants and do me?"

Too Hot

"I can't perform under these conditions," Chops said. "Cross my heart and hope to die. If I'm lyin, you can take this money I collected and buy yourself a little engine that can."

Chops pulled out a doo-rag and wiped his face as it grew plump from the heat.

"Just give me some old-fashioned love," said Zu-Zu. "I want hanky-panky."

Chops wanted to do Zu-Zu to stretch his pants but wasn't confident he had the skills to do her. He stood still and tried to catch his breath while niggas came up and offered to do Zu-Zu for him.

They Got To Go

"I want to be the only one who gets it," Chops said to Zu-Zu.

"Okay, okay, okay," said Zu-Zu. "I'm a mighty tight woman. Do me in a place where it's warm and where your hooch won't turn bad. I don't care where you take it."

Paradise

"Behind the garbage," said Chops. "Seven steps to Heaven."

Chops pulled out a bomb and lit it, weed all in Zu-Zu's face, smoke getting in her eyes. Zu-Zu started singing "Dope Head Blues," Chops high as a kite.

"Give me that old slow drag," said Zu-Zu.

Chops gave Zu-Zu the bomb, and she sucked on the edges of it until it exploded in her mouth. She spat the paper out and the ashes came out, too, like her mouth was a volcano.

"Spit in the sky and it fall in your eye," Chops said.

"That nigga is just gonna drag you down," I said to Zu-Zu.

Chops glared at me, his eyes like obsidian pieces. "What's that supposed to mean?" he asked.

"Don't ask me, Chops," I said. "I'm just a jitterbug. When I hear music, it makes me dance."

Zu-Zu became restless. She started singing "Tired of Waiting Blues."

"I'm dying by the hour," said Zu-Zu.

"She's gotta have it," I told Chops.

"Knees up, Zu-Zu," Chops said. Then Chops fell down and pounced on top of her stomach. Zu-Zu spat in his face.

"Bring back the joys," said Zu-Zu. She reminisced to the days when she usta' hang with "Madame Walker," homegirl who threw all these wild parties in her home, affectionately called the "Dark Tower." A'Lelia Walker was so freaky that niggas called her "joy goddess of Harlem." Zu-Zu kicked it with Madame Walker until one day some treacherous gangsta girls — toss-ups servicing male gang members — jumped her on 136th Street to prove that they could handle theirs. Madame Walker was robbed and stabbed over 19 times. The heat had melted the black comb in her hand by the time the blues found her in the street. Once pushed into the street, Zu-Zu started drinking more bitters and airing out all of her dirty laundry.

"I'm a mean, tight mama," said Zu-Zu, staring straight into Chops' face.

Chops slung off his leather and whipped her. The

17

scorching and burning and fire straightened Zu-Zu's rough and nappy hair like Madame Walker's hot comb. With a bottle of moonshine in his big, black hands, Chops looked like Prince Buster trying to make love to Zu-Zu, pastry crumbs all over her lips like caviar and ashes still coming out of her mouth. Use your imagination.

"Ooh!" she screamed. "Oh Carolina! Olcum!" She called out Yoko Ono's name as well, then made even her mouth the shape of an O.

Chops ran Zu-Zu along the wood while she moaned, grunted, huffed and puffed and blew into his bottle, making it blown glass.

Two niggas heavy on the bottle, Flukie and Sterling Silver, staggered by together carrying a stolen television set as Zu-Zu kicked over the garbage can. They went crazy.

"This brother is tearing this hooch up!" shouted Flukie as if he was dropping some serious science, his mouth full of gold fillings, just the plastic wrapper of a Hostess Twinkie in his pockets.

"I wish I had some of that, baby doll," Sterling said.

"You can get it if you really want, Bro-ham," said Zu-Zu.

Chops held out the bottle. "It's almost all gone," said Chops. Flukie and Sterling Silver dropped the television set, ran over and snatched the bottle out of Chops' hand. Meantime, Zu-Zu looked 'em up and down.

"Dang girl, you sho' is big," said Flukie and Sterling simultaneously. They were willing to say anything when it came to a woman. "Look at you, girl. Your breasts are African grapes. Your stuff is all over the place."

Chops clung to the bottle and pushed them back, away from Zu-Zu, whom he considered his to make over.

"Take your black bottom out of here!" Zu-Zu cried.

"Go home!" Chops shouted.

In the mean time, Zu-Zu pushed the buttons on the television set to see if she could find the news that would tell about the negro world.

"Keep going!" Chops shouted.

Long Road

"Which way do we go?" asked Flukie, his hand directly over his cock. Sterling followed suit.

"Follow the beaten path," I said. They looked at me like I was a trip.

"It's a long walk home!" they shouted. Chops gave them the finger.

They cracked up and then kissed Chops' black ass goodbye. "See ya' lata (chee, chee)."

Walkin

With a cock-of-the-walk stride, Flukie and Sterling Silver passed through gun smoke on the way to get out of Dodge, two car jackers doing a job within earshot from where they left Zu-Zu scrambling to pick up her stuff, Chops on top of her doing a Spike Lee joint with his finger, the whole scene like something you'd find in Crooklyn.

Flukie felt the urge to shine Sterling's head. Sterling wondered whether or not Flukie was good luck. Both men were bluing, unable to get their hands on moonshine or Kool-Aid or Grape Juice or anything that looked like it could have alcohol content.

Flukie fell out. "It's a dizzy atmosphere," he said.

Sterling said nothing as they passed a monk standing in a puddle at the corner and dipping while drinking moonshine.

"Don't stand in muddy waters," said Flukie, out of it. "Dig?"

"I'm bad," said Monk.

Sterling Silver, in a moment of epiphany, pointed at Monk's socks. He was floodin'.

Flukie tried to play it off. "What's that in yo' pocket?" Flukie asked.

"Watches," said Monk, "from yo' momma."

Flukie started to tag him. But, Sterling Silver held him back.

"How much they cost?" asked Sterling Silver. He and Flukie would turn against their own mothers for blood money.

"Sell out," said Monk. "They not for sell, nigga."

"Then what is you selling?" Flukie asked.

"Time," said Monk. "I stole the watches from Penney's so I could give a brother time. You ain't got to buy any, but if you don't I'll take you out."

Flukie and Sterling Silver looked at one another and backed up.

"You ain't that bad," said Flukie.

"You not superfly," said Sterling Silver.

"You ain't one of those naked lady statues with wings perched on the hood of a caddy."

"You not the 'son of badd' either."

"You ain't some superhero."

"You not like Coffee."

"Sho' ain't Christie Love."

"Not Cleopatra Jones either."

"Or me and Mrs. Jones."

"You got a thang going on, but nobody wants any part of yours, homeboy."

"Ain't nobody gonna be calling you Shaft, my brother."

"Not you."

"You more like Mead on *Mandingo*."

"Raw, like Eddie Murphy."

"You belong on *Comic View*."

"Cause you pry more than Richard Pryor."

"You might want to try *Showtime at the Apollo*."

"I don't recommend Ed Small's Sugar Cane Club at 135th Street and Fifth Avenue."

"But the Cotton Club on Lenox Avenue ain't bad."

"You qualify as a Harlem experimental player."

"Why don't you give Bethel African Methodist Episcopal Church a try?" said Flukie.

Monk stepped closer on the beaten path and stared right into Sterling Silver's crooked eyes. "Gentlemen," he said, showing them the watches, the hands moving like drunks. "Your time is almost out."

"You don't know nothing!" Sterling Silver shouted, his face all shiny while he looked around out of the corner of his eye for a fork on the ground to use as a weapon.

"You just a pusher," said Flukie.

"I'm yo' pusher," replied Monk. "Pay me, niggas, or I'll close yo' big lips forever."

Flukie pinched Sterling Silver's arm. "We should have stayed behind with the hoochie momma," he said.

Sterling Silver cleaned his throat, then spoke up. "What do you know about karate?" he asked, notorious for his stereotyping based on people's names.

"Jujitsu," said Monk. "Before I studied the art, a punch to me was just a punch, a kick was just a kick. After I studied the art, a punch was no longer a punch, a kick no longer a kick. Now that I understand the art, a punch is a punch, a kick is just a kick."

"Damn, I'm a big nigga, but you got me scared," said Flukie.

21

"Um, excuse me, Mr. Monk," said Sterling, "but I have a question. That's some deep shit you just gave us. Are you from the temple of Shaolin? Or, is that from the tao of jeet kune do? Or what?"

"If nothing within you stays rigid, outward things will disclose themselves," said Monk. "Moving, be like water. Still, be like a mirror. Respond like an echo."

"Don't make us bust you up," said Flukie. But, he was only faking. Truth is, he was scared and didn't know what else to do, so he resorted to trash talking.

"The softest thing cannot be snapped," replied Monk. He sat down and folded his legs, determined to walk away with at least bitches' brew.

"Man, why don't you take a chill pill, come and get blowed with us?" Flukie asked, like he knew for sure Monk was a high roller.

"Humph," said Monk. "We're no longer on Monk's time. I got no papers. Plus, LuLu's back in town."

"What you want?" Sterling Silver asked. "Oriental? Ramen Noodles? Chinese spare ribs? Rice cakes for Father?"

Monk set his drink down and stood up again. "Die hard," he said.

Flukie backed up even more. "Don't mess wit me," warned Flukie. "I'll rock your world."

"You're time is out," said Monk. "And after I get through wit you, I'm going back to find the skeezer and get her, too."

Someday My Prince Will Come

said Zu-Zu. "But, you sure as hell ain't him."

Chops exploded. He let go of his bomb and slid Zu-Zu from left to right on the wood, putting splinters into the blackest cracks in her skin. Zu-Zu screamed, caught in the middle of a wang-dang with her face under cork.

"Ooh!" she screamed. "Oh Carolina. Olcum." She threw in "Olive Oyl" for good measure.

Chops grabbed an empty bottle and held it over his big head, Zu-Zu moaning and groaning and asking "Can Anybody Take Sweet Mama's Place?"

In Case of Emergency, Break Glass

I rushed over and tapped the bottle against Chops' head. Chops looked at me like I was crazy, pieces of glass snagged inside his afro, blue rain dripping down his black forehead.

"Non de guerre," Chops said. He squeezed his head with his fingers. "Peace out," he added. Then he fell flat on his fat face, smashing his cheeks up against the rest of the bench.

Yelling, I took off. Zu-Zu picked up her boob-tube and spat on the back of Chops' head. "My handy man ain't handy no more," she said.

She pointed at the stuff running down the side of his face. "Save the juice," she said to him, like he could hear her.

I'm Always Chasing Rainbows

Zu-Zu continued shouting and crying. "One minute, they there. The next minute, they gone."

Miles in the Sky

"Baby, you send me," said Monk. "When you fall short of love, it will be forever." Monk reached into his dashiki or kimono or whatever it was, pulled out two nigger flickers and put the primitive blades together to suggest scissors. He gave Flukie's big head the evil eye.

Flukie squinted at the sight of the metal, which he imagined as being from the inside of Slice cans. He tried to play everything off. "Kronka," he said. It meant "let the games begin."

Sterling Silver was at the top of an elm tree, singing "Freddy's Dead," brothers throwing down fishbone a couple

23

of trees farther away, the whole thing a nightmare.

"Man, can't we all just get along?" asked one cat.

"Yeah, is that alright with you?"

"Why you doing us like this?"

"There's too many fine chicks walkin' around for us to be in the treetops."

"If you going to kill somebody, kill the nigga and come on."

"Do him in first-degree murder."

"Special circumstances."

"Castrate him so you can show him who's the master."

"Use the body parts for Chinese spareribs."

"Cut and mix."

"Do it til you satisfied."

"Drain the blood out like it were black cherry Kool-Aid."

"Make sure you leave no loose juice behind."

"Nigga, you can be Blacula."

"It ain't enough to play night-stalker."

"We just squirrels trying to get a nut, but, with respect, you could have all the flesh you want."

"Dip into anybody's Kool-Aid without knowing the flavor."

"Aa-a, bat around."

"Nobody could stop you, baby."

"Call me Bernard Wright."

"Al B. Sure!"

"It's obvious that, with a body on your rep, you could be tall."

"Take the chance, baby."

"I would if I could."

"Cut the crap, then go back where you fell."

"It ain't nothin' but a G-thang, baby."

"You just stepped into the comfort zone."

"Do whatever you feel like, what turns you on."

"We up here in the trees hollywood swingin'."

"Always wanted to see the cool and the gang show."

"Go ahead, make our day."

"Get off."

"Yeah, yeah."

"Turn this mutha out."

"Let's get it started."

"We got high hopes, but we're not the S.O.S. band."

"That's fo' damn sure."

"No one's gonna love you."

"We don't care enough to stop you."

"Can't find the reasons."

"But we know you can do no bad by yo' self."

"Look at the man in the mirror."

"You got to do the right thing."

"But whatever you do, won't you make up your mind?"

"Shut up!" screamed Monk. He stabbed a tree behind Flukie's big head.

Flukie stepped back. "Give me tonight," he said.

From the top of the elm tree, Sterling Silver lowered his cotton handkerchief and long gold rope chain. "Hang him high," he said to Flukie.

As if on cue, niggas in the trees stuck their heads out of the branches and started talking smack again, grown men gossiping like women, twigs falling to the ground like hairpins. Some niggas were crying as if they were at a wake.

"Look around you," said Sterling. "What you want? You can have anything you want. Ain't no stoppin' you now."

"I need love," said Monk. "I want an around-the-way girl. I want base."

25

"We all do," said Flukie.

"But a nigga round here got to be careful work that sucka to the bone," said Sterling Silver.

"Around the way, I saw a hottie, no thicker than a twig, but with big titties," said Flukie.

"Let us walk, and we'll make a special delivery," said Sterling.

"Yo' call," said Flukie.

"Titties taste like watermelons," said Sterling.

"Make her come my way," said Monk. He told Flukie and Sterling to pucker while he gave them a shot. Of his moonshine. "You better not try to run, or the chickens will come home to roost," he said.

"I thought you'd see it my way," said Flukie. He gulped whiskey and heard niggas tripping, his head starting to ache.

"What's all this noise?" Flukie asked.

"The sounds of 52nd Street," said Sterling, swallowing whiskey from the cup as if he had found the Grail.

Flukie and Sterling took off, one step closer to Heaven.

South Street Exit

Miles ahead.

Blue Gray

All the way to downtown, people celebrate, Linton Johnson splashing rhythms together after the thundering bass in Central Park. Unfortunately, in the middle of the party, there is a Blue Vein Circle, in the shady area of the park, where mulattoes and light-skin blacks practice color snobbery and diss "darkies." Johnson is toasting with a mike in his hand. "The earth has music for those who listen," he says, pointing toward a black man fondling his girl, an overweight white chick, on a bench. "This is Tabu."

Johnson steps over to a set of 1200 turntables and a Gemini

mixer and stops the wax with his fingers. Still on the microphone, he does his own play-by-play: "The rhythms jus bubbling an back-firing, ragin and rising, then suddenly the music cuts — steel blade drinking blood in darkness." He points again at the black-and-white couple, the Blue Vein Circle.

"It's war amongst the rebels," says Johnson. "What we need is dread, beat, an' blood." He's scratching the lines of the skin on two old cuts, repeating "dread at the control" and "it's time." Girls love the way Johnson spins, many of them leaning over the DJ table with a J in their mouths.

Johnson is trying hard not to get the big head. "I don't want to be like Bob Marley," he says. He's got a bomb in his mouth bigger than the mike in his hands.

With all the noise and fanfare (the park is packed with party people), Chops wakes up and tries to remix Johnson's speech in order to get attention. "I don't want to be chop suey," he screams, rolling over to where Johnson is doing his thang, leather skirts all up in his face.

Johnson grins and steps on Chops with his combat boots. Women scream.

"I refuse to divorce myself from the realities of life," says Johnson.

"I don't want to be chopped liver either. Living in the bottle where everything is distorted or distilled."

Johnson kicks Chops in the mouth. "Everybody's got to find their own groove," says Johnson. "You a sorry case, if you can't."

He holds his black thang and scratches it in front of the ladies.

His beat is so fonky: Men holler, "It's sweet as a nut—just level vibes."

Chops pulls his upper lip away from a cleat and, like Zu-Zu, spits the dirt out of his mouth. Suddenly, he's starting to gain a little more respect for Johnson.

"Let the beat hit 'em!" Chops shouts. "Let the music take control! Let the beat go round and round and up and down!"

Then Johnson kicks the ballistics, and Chops in the head, and walks away. Chops is knocked out again.

Johnson is downright unfaithful. Some meddling reporters from the liberal side of print media follow him as if in a golf tournament. They fight to see him, cutting out each other's hearts and giving them to dippers with paper asses and buckets of blood. Everyone is high on brew or drawing a pound or two of kally, Johnson passin' naturals on niggas. Emulating him, a quartet of black boys stand in the weed and hold their dicks in front of a 35mm camera from *Rolling Stone* looking for real gangsta rappers; some people in the hood describe the teenagers as niggas-with-an-attitude—Dr. Dre, Easy E, Ice Cube and MC Ren carbon copies shooting simply to promote the idea of being "niggas 4 life." Truth is, they even scare the photographer, who exposes his film to light. In the mean time, the ugly black boy that people compare to Easy E is even crying (whining) like him, breathing with difficulty.

I Wanna Thank You (For Letting Me Be Myself)

I told God. I told him good.

"God," I said. "God, please don't let me spend the rest of my life in a park. If you gotta take me, take me to higher ground. But please don't let me go in the park. Please don't let me go in park."

"God," I said. "I know you are the man. You definitely be the stuff. You sure is the man. I want muscles."

I gazed around at New York.

Pretty City

But it wasn't the promised land.

Speedy shortstop Shawon Dunston grew up in Brooklyn. Everybody talked about how fast he was. Niggas bragged about how they had his back. Then Dunston hurt himself playing in the major leagues. Some said it because he was too fast, got himself out there. Whatever the case, nobody talks about him anymore.

There was also Edmund Perry. His momma should have never called him "Edmund" from the get-go. It sounds like a little spoiled British boy from *The Lion, The Witch* and *The Wardrobe*. I read that book once, but it had too much fantasy. You can't find fantasy in Harlem. But anyway, Eddie Perry was another nigga from around-the-way. Smart, but liked too many white girls, thought he was Richie Rich. After Eddie moved the crowd to go to Exeter prep school, he was shot by a white cop in street clothes and quit it. The blues killed Eddie Perry: It was even rumored by "angels" that Father Divine predicted they couldn't live long.

Murder In The First Degree

said Zu-Zu. "You shall reap what you sow."

"Maybe," I said, "but I can't be no ordinary Mo. I got to get out of the ghetto, too. If I live by tripping, at least I did it my way." I got this Frank Sinatra song in my head.

After hitting Chops on the head with a bottle and wandering away, I was not surprised to return to the area and find Chops appearing dead; when you're black, you get used to expecting the worse.

After first looking at each other, me and Zu-Zu stared down at Chops on the grass; he continued to show no signs of movement. Zu-Zu rolled Chops over and spat in his face.

"He got it good and that ain't bad," said Zu-Zu. "You

29

chopped his fat head into pieces."

"Sing sing prison,"

"Someday, Sweetheart," answered Zu-Zu.

After Tonight

I said, "I'm a dead man."

I covered Chops' body with a blanket. Zu-Zu spat once more in his face.

"Excuse me, pardon me, don't let me get in your way," I said to Zu-Zu. "But this ain't East Harlem or Staten Island or Tribeca or Brooklyn. This downtown, at least for drifting niggas. And we way down. You just can't go around spitting in niggas' faces. I ain't eighty-sixin no more niggas for you. Dig?"

Zu-Zu cracked up. "I killed him first," she said. "Don't you forget that."

As I mumbled "Soho," she pulled a set of lines out of her shoe that looked like Chops' forehead peeled from the bottom of her foot and did a little number.

"I am the laughing woman with the black black face," said Zu-Zu.

"Lighten up, honey," I said.

"Living in cellars and in every crowded place."

"Get it together."

"I am toiling just to eat," she says.

"When life gets cheesy, you put on the Ritz."

"And I laugh," said Zu-Zu.

"You got your independent funk, Zu-Zu. It's fine and dandy, except don't you forget one thing either. You ain't a grown woman yet. Don't forget how you ran away from the crib several times before you finally escaped, taking baby breaths. All this before you started hangin' with Madame Walker, who schooled you on men. At least, this is what you told me and Chops before."

"Why you gotta call me out?" Zu-Zu asked. She scooted over on the bench "My daddy likes it slow," she said.

"You don't know what love is," I told Zu-Zu.

"Sweet rain," she said.

"Things ain't what they used to be," I said. I dreamed of chocolate kisses, mumbling.

"Such sweet thunder," Zu-Zu whispered in my ear.

I quickly tried to move away from Zu-Zu. Her heart was a singing bird, a prelude to Charlie Parker. Everytime her arms fluttered, her attempted embrace gave me Flack—"The Closer I Get To You," "Oasis" or "The First Time Ever I Saw Your Face."

"What are you singing this time, Zu-Zu?"

"The Song Is You," she answered.

"What's wrong with 'Paper Moon' or 'Kind of Blue' or 'Hand Jive' or 'Emotions' or 'Forms and Sounds' or 'Anatomy of Murder' or 'Sara Smile' or 'I Don't Know What Kind of Blues I've Got' or 'Dat Dere'?" I asked.

"No more talk," said Zu-Zu. "For me, life is like the black plague, houses and houses of hoochie mommas in Bedford-Stuyvesant full of disease that the white man carries back home to Bensonhurst, Queens, and gives to his wife."

"We're bigger than life, Zu-Zu."

"When women talk that way, we die," said Zu-Zu, her lips dark.

Mood Indigo

All we ever do is talk, but it seems like everything we say is dead—flatliners. The world keeps right on spinning, twisting and turning, without us. Zu-Zu says we are nothing more than cheap labor.

"I can't do no more," says Zu-Zu. She's lying her ass off.

"Hush, girl, be quiet," I say.

If I Could Save Time In A Bottle

Zu-Zu got a bottle in her hands and a river of booze running from the big mouth to the thin black lining inside her stomach. It rained for hours in the park before night hit our faces and covered our skin like an umbrella, but not before giving us the watery blues. I wore the mask, Zu-Zu dragging me through the mud, everyone celebrating and stomping on muddy waters even after the thrill was gone. Spooks turned into faded boogies. The only thing distinctly visible was the bleeding lips of undaunted pretty women, the kind that believe a make-up kit is the answer to everything.

The small trees in the park were bent or down, dropped by big niggas and east rains that slashed their heads, arms, and legs like it was nothing. During the parade of storms, the trees shook and danced in the wind, their leaves like damaged hair washed with no soap and black dirty water.

New York stood tall as a mob city with a mouth the size of Frank Sinatra's. Zu-Zu and I sat on the bench, our shoes heavy with mud, and ate crab apples, Zu-Zu's stomach wining and dining her until she finally belched. Zu-Zu threw down the last apple. Feeling her stomach—feeling sick, she nervously swung her feet, then dug one of her shoes into the black soil, her sole in deep and the other one seemingly crying way inside her dark belly.

New York was an overcrowded place trumped up by the rich and powerful and the media, its central location being a Jurassic Park where men and women ate alone in public and nobody talked. Zu-Zu smoked a cigarette from the garbage and blew cool mint in my face. Then, she spat pieces of cigarette paper out in the sky as if she were throwing up a fistful of dollars.

Zu-Zu reached inside her blouse, wondering if she had any money left. I continued to sit on the bench, even the Kool contemplating between my fingers while I sung "Woman, don't you know with you, I'm born again."

I felt it was time she knew.

"Time," I told her.

"Time," she stopped.

With New York comparable to Guatemala or Haiti in terms of the overwhelming number of homeless people and children out on the street, nobody dared to talk. They feared the blues. The cops seemed to murder, rape, beat, or set up anyone who openly protested against the White House. ("Paint the White House black," suggested some migrant southern nigga who, when he said it, was living around the way. His idea was dismissed when someone pointed out that he never did look up from the ground. And, even his own cousin added that he was afraid of the dollar bill because it had The Man's face on it.)

But anyway, Zu-Zu actually told me to shut up. She even stopped swinging.

"No more dancing girl, Zu-Zu?"

Zu-Zu shook her head, "No." She pulled a handgun out of the garbage can where she stored her stuff and raised it to her head.

Black Monday was the first day of autumn. The fall season came with a bang.

Zu-Zu dropped to the ground and fell out.

"Toy gun," said Zu-Zu. She cracked up. She showed me the black plastic handle.

"When you fall, get up," I said. I handed Zu-Zu some fire, and we burned while she ran her broken acrylic fingernails through the grass.

33

Purple Haze

I sucked my joint, blue-faced, dragging like Jimi Hendrix with a guitar pick hanging over a bottomed-out lip. In the moist night air, we smoked all the grass we could find. Nigger heaven became a smoked-up black skillet holding the earth together, my girl Zu-Zu toiling in the soil though she really wasn't my girl. The clouds around our faces were pasta-red. Like mobsters, we sucked on reefers as if they were puffy spaghetti and macaroni.

As we looked beyond the haze, everything seemed blue. The earth was shapeless, chaotic mass with the spirit of God brooding over the dark vapors, niggas strutting around on The Chronic and dressed like starving artists. Some super thin brother even claimed he did J.J.'s paintings in *Good Times*; he swore that the lighted bomb in his mouth was dynomite.

I watched the brother stagger away, then turned and looked at Zu-Zu. Like the rest, she was dope and stir-crazy.

Nefertiti

There was swinging on 52nd Street. Zu-Zu listened for it in pursuit of the 27th man. I heard only the echo of Phil Collins somewhere singing "she calls out to the man on the street."

Defiantly still sitting down, Zu-Zu crossed her legs like she was the queen of Harlem, the primary bee in everybody's business. She believed she was royalty and would not allow anyone to break her spirit. She made it a point to consistently remind me that she was from Queens and would have still been there had she not decided to run away for good.

"Whenever you try to do good, evil is always pressing," I once said. Zu-Zu just gave me the look, and, for the first time, I realized that I had been missing the point. Zu-Zu always told me, "Just because you have been married doesn't mean you're in love." After sneaking and peeping Zu-Zu's diary in

34

the park, I found out that she had "escaped" from her parents. Although her saying always sounded like something she had stole from Rick James, I knew that she was bold like that:

Straight Hincty

Once on a downright unfaithful and violent night after James Brown gave her his barbecue rib in a Harlem hotel room, Zu-Zu Girl, still thinking about what happened to Madame Walker, decided to comb the real kinky streets of the city to find a better home and garden than the one she had with this low-down cheesy "player" named Sa-Sa she was screwing in a condemned office building behind his honky wife's back.

Singing "Leaving You Baby" on her way to the subway, she stopped on the sidewalk talk to peep the window of a black-owned store, even her shadow blue. She saw Rap's *Die Nigger Die* on sale. Girl almost tripped out. She pounded the window, her black black face occasionally pressing against the glass, her bare feet accidentally wiping the dirty names off the graffiti where she stood. Customers went in and out, but no one paid her any attention.

So in front of the window, Zu-Zu pulled out a bomb and lit it, the cigarette leaning on the corner of her mouth like a hooker, a black cloud hanging around her and the nigger joint. Between smokes, she paused and waited for men to pass by so she could kick up dirt in their faces.

"Get yo' black face out of the window!" the fat owner of the store finally shouted, his black-and-white television showing *Cops* where Charlie Irvine is on the freeway beating and arresting a buck-naked brown African American who is staring into the camera like a deer in headlights waiting to be hit.

Zu-Zu blew the store owner a death kiss and let the lipstick bleeding on his window tell him that he had just got himself involved with a horror/whore.

Like Zu-Zu's Uncle Tom before he molested her, the store owner tucked in his white shirt and approached the door, his big black hand still feeling on his Fruit-of-the-Loom and Boyz II Men's song "Uhh-Ahh" on his mind.

Zu-Zu pointed at his body. "You livin' large," she said.

"Get away from the window!" he answered. "You'll bust the glass with yo' bean head, and I'd have to get in yo' stuff for sure then! You'd be screaming 'bout how I hurt you." He pointed to her loose skirt being blown between her thighs by the nasty wind.

Zu-Zu spat on the window. He gave her the finger. "You little mustard face, pumpkinhead, devil-bitch," he said. "Get away from the window before you break it and end up gettin' yourself hurt like that LaTasha Harlins girl!" He grabbed his crotch and told her to stay if she wanted some.

"I'm a private dancer," Zu-Zu yelled, "dancin' for money. But someday, I'll take you out, sweetheart. Someday."

Zu-Zu spat once more on the glass and then moved the crowd and blended her black face in with the inner city blues, all of it making her wanna holler.

Zu-Zu Girl beat the rocks. She flew toward the subway like a bluebird, her sole/soul all cut up from the time she spent on the curb.

While marching down Martin Luther King Boulevard, she heard a lot of footsteps in the dark, niggas running around and destroying housing projects in the wake of the Rodney King beating, the wind pushing trash up to her feet.

When Zu-Zu heard the roar of an approaching subway train, she started flying back towards the King street, the black train drowning her screams, kissing her booty goodbye.

Even if Zu-Zu had been Vanessa Williams singing "Can This Be Real," she wouldn't have won any Miss America beauty contests the way she carried on. But just because she screamed and cried and hollered all the way down the street like she was having a baby, it didn't mean that she was weak. She was scared for her life, which for her was nothing but a walking shadow but somebody had to protect it.

Since she wasn't rich or white enough to own a Sprint calling card that could save her life in a pay phone, Zu-Zu threw herself into an alley that ended with a fence and stood there hot, the chain link calling her and poking at her behind her back, feeling her booty like it had never had any before. With the fence against her, Girl waited for her attacker. She was ready to do him, squeezing the end of a nigger-flicker in her right hand that would chop him down to size.

"Come and get it, Bro-ham," she said.

After a group of black teenage boys ran past the entrance of the alley, Sa-Sa finally approached her directly, where she could see him. He wore black leather boots that came up to his knee and had large heels. His polyester shirt was unbuttoned, the hairs on his chest like sutures where women's long, painted fingernails had tore up his chest and stomach and he had tried to put himself back together. He fired up a joint and blew foul smoke in Zu-Zu's face, charbroiling her lips and nose into gall. With an attitude, Zu-Zu watched him cop and blow. He shook his jheri-curl in front of her, spraying sweet-smelling glycerin and Sta-Sof in her face. Then he pushed her further up against the fence.

"When I came to yo' place of business last night," he said, "you wouldn't even talk to me. Then I find out in the street you've been chasin' other niggas like a little groupie." He pulled out a tired 45 vinyl single of "Big Payback" and stuck the chipped edge of it in her throat, the record's red label bleeding onto the black skin.

"Sa-Sa, that ain't me," Zu-Zu said, only reneging to wait for the right moment. "You got the wrong girl."

"Shut up!" he said. "Bitches ain't shit but hoes and tricks." He blew weed up her nose.

Zu-Zu closed her nose, asked him to step off, pushed him back, and showed him the nigger-flicker, pointing the rough razor at his nipples.

Blood peeped his unbuttoned shirt and rushed to his brain begging him to forget about her.

"Shut up!" he yelled again. "I'm bustin' out, and I don't give a damn. If you don't like my funk, then take yo' stuff and scram."

Zu-Zu Girl appeared to have rotten squash for breasts but did the best she could to flaunt it, set 'em out. "Come and get it," she said.

He laughed: "Do I look stupid and on food stamps (sa, sa, sa, sa, sa)? You come over here and give it to me, baby."

Sa-Sa continually used the food stamps in Zu-Zu's face. He constantly told her that before she met him she had nothing but paper money. Zu-Zu later confessed that she didn't do him because he was brilliant or something; she said it was all the money stuff that got to her.

"Lovin' you ain't easy cause you're beautiful," said Zu Zu, laughing back, her voice like Minnie Riperton singing "la, la, la, la, la." "You ain't too far gone to see that yet. Why you trying to pretend like this is a stage? You ain't no performer. I've been to hundreds and thousands of speakeasies before and you the only one I've ever seen that didn't belong there."

Blood sucked dope and laughed as if in a Jason Voorhees'

horror/whore film: "(Sa, sa, sa, sa) I'm in love with Mary Jane," he said. "She's my main thang. It comes as no surprise. She takes me to paradise."

Standing on a heap of trash, Zu-Zu spread her legs against the chain link like a slave. "Come on, baby, come into my house," she said.

He smacked Girl across the bridge of her nose. She felt pain like the bridge had been reconstructed.

"I'm cold-blooded," he said.

"Then today is a good day," said Zu-Zu. She stabbed him with the knife, for A'Lelia, and for her mother, who also died in the hands of a man, and for her mother's mother, who was severed in half in 1925 when her abusive husband chased her down in the street and whipped her, then whacked her on the head with a bottle and placed her on a railroad line — with young boys running alongside the tracks shouting, a train carrying Dutch Master's cigars liberated him. It was said that, though no one could tell for sure, many folks believed that she died with a fag in her mouth and clutching her papers, just like a tired runaway Negress slave. After the woman's defeat, young black women and mammies protested by using the entrails of cut-up chickens to etch chicken scratch on the man's beat-up truck.

With the idea of attaining freedom at all costs, Zu-Zu tried to kill the man. But Sa-Sa had been stabbed so many times before he met Zu-Zu until he simply forgot. Blood grabbed her hand and cracked up, the chain link still feeling her soft booty, her mascara running.

He approached her breasts like a rapist, a neurotic who takes things into his own hands. She kicked his rocks. He cracked up and kicked her back near the vagina, fragments of crack falling by his foot and out of his dope cigarette.

She gathered herself and spat in his face. He wiped off the saliva and stuck out his tongue. She slit it.

Blood looked surprised. He fell to his knees and released her from the chain. She carved a small hole in his big head, wrote on a piece of paper, and inserted a note that said "don't fuck with a Girl."

Then she took off his baggies and shirt and long gold triple key chain, and, with a tube of red lipstick, drew on the pavement an outline of a human figure sprawled out. She rolled his black body inside the drawing. The look was trendy, in fashion with the lifestyles of the poor and non-famous.

It was only by coincidence that the coppers saw her. They were happily doing their routine. They parked their white squad car on King Boulevard, slowly walked down the alley and asked her what happened, holding their sticks in front of Zu-Zu.

Her blouse all open and hovering over the body like a buzzard's, Zu-Zu elevated her bird chest and straightened up to fly right since it was her word against the deceased.

"I tried to stop him, boys," said Zu-Zu. "After he attacked me with this primitive nigger-flicker while I was strolling and singing "Livin' Humble," I sprayed him with a can of bug spray, but he kept coming, cussin' and swearin' like a blind splib or butter head or member snapping. 'Shut up!' he said, trying to cover my mouth. In self-defense, I grabbed the knife out of his hand and sliced off his big lips, silencing him forever. I was sitting, just coolin', waiting for the police, when a large group of gang-bangers came by, robbed him and finished him for good, took what they wanted from me, and drew an outline around his lazy ass as a joke to suggest that the murder was premeditated. Don't look at me. I swear."

"Is that the best I'm-not-a-crook monologue you can give?" the coppers asked. They dragged her down the alley by her wrists and hair.

"If the Mayor could see us now," chuckled one. As her butt scraped and skipped across the ground, Zu-Zu saw a large button bouncing on his shirt pocket that said "proud to be a Republican."

When they got back to the entrance of the alley, the same one stopped and stared through the rain accompanying the white gusting winds of the storm: "Niggers sure do hate the water, don't they?"

Zu-Zu fought off the urge to spit in his face. She wasn't seddity or conservative enough to fuss if a black person called his or her homey a "nigger," but she hated it when a white man used the word. That's just the way it was. I guess it was a black thang.

"Where you think you're taking me?" she asked him.

"Sing sing prison."

"Then you can have a catbird seat all by yourself," the other one added.

"Now that you're with New York's finest, exercise your right to remain silent," they said. "If you don't do what we want, this might be the last time you're ever gonna see Soul City and its shady places."

Zu-Zu spat in their piggish faces, carefully reaching into the elasticity of her skirt for the nigger-flicker while the coppers were looking to see where her spittle had gone.

They pushed her big head into the car, laughing, holding on to their guns.

"Show-time," said one of the coppers, getting into the car with her, his red, white, and blue button bouncing up-and down. quickly, he stripped his watch and stashed it away in

41

his pants pocket, nervously digging up the rubber on the floor. The other one searched the front seat for popcorn, then turned around to peep as if it were time for the show to begin. Zu-Zu faked hollering and screaming, the knife by her side, the black woman vowing "no justice, no peace/piece" in a low voice hushed inside the squad car. The blues closely surrounded Zu-Zu while King leaned over the car, ruined, shaking violently—like a punk-ass drum major in the middle passage letting the white man know when to stroke.

Love Is Strange

"I'm not a king—I'm just a guy," I told Zu-Zu, still standing up, too scared to sit down. Even the rain had decided to be silent.

"That's the main reason," she said, "that I will never forgive your treacherous ass. You are the man who violated my privacy." She removed her dirty shoe, threw it like a spitball pitcher, and hit me near the eye with it. "What you looking at?"

Embarrassed, I once again sucked the joint dying in-between my soft fingers. I turned around and bent over, blue-faced, dragging like Jim Hendrix, my lip bottomed out seemingly for good, nothing around us but sirens, bright lights, and big-ass ghetto-birds, some niggas apparently trying to fade one another several yards away but still right in front of our faces. Chops was still out, the blanket hugging his large shoulders, Zu-Zu mashing down the mud cloth with her other foot so he couldn't rise up.

"Think you could ever love a man, Zu-Zu?" I stopped moving and finally looked her straight in the eye.

"What do you think?"

"I thought maybe you could love me."

Zu-Zu looked me straight in the eye, then cackled: Sh i-

i-i-i-i-i-tt!" she said. "Nigga, you must be out of your mind.
I ain't no dark lady or Alice in Wonderland or Sweet Sue
honey or chicken dumpling or Daisy Wheel or pork fritter or
Anita Baker for you to have...think again."

"It takes two to make a thing go right," I said. "Didn't your
parents ever whip you or give you some guidance?"

"My mother was weak," Zu-Zu answered, "like you, judg-
ing from what you've shown me so far. And my daddy was
mean to the point where nobody could talk to him. With
lightweight gloves on his fists, he beat my mother, then
shouted 'I'm the greatest.' While in the military, he buried
a broomstick in the ass of a homosexual. And then after the
Vietnam War, he said he ripped out the eye of his dumb-ass
cousin Horrus, walked it to the graveyard, and 'set it on top
of a coffin so that the dead may see again.' And if he were
here tonight, he'd probably screw a sissy like you with his
middle finger."

"I don't think so. Yo' daddy's love for graphic violence
makes him a prime candidate for HBO, that is, have-not
blown out-of-the-way."

"You better think," said Zu-Zu. "You ain't got enough
heart. You couldn't take out my daddy if you were producing
a HBO Special. When I left the crib for good, I whispered
'goodbye, heartache.'" Zu-Zu paused. "It could have been
'good morning.'"

Stella By Starlight

"Now was it 'goodbye' or 'good morning'?" I had to know.

"It was blue cellophane over my nose and mouth, easy
living, my foolish heart, a frame for the blues," Zu-Zu
answered. She was referring to life with her family before the
escape.

"What did you say when you left that hot house?" I asked.

43

"I sung 'It's So Hard To Say Goodbye To Yesterday,'" said Zu- Zu.

Zu-Zu stood to straighten herself. It was like watching a nudie flick. She deliberately stuck her foot in the small of Chops' back and kicked it while he was unconscious. "This is the point of no return," she said. Then she kicked him again in the same point.

"You got a lot of nerve, Zu-Zu." I had no idea what she was doing.

Zu-Zu started strutting around before picking a yellow umbrella out of the trash and opening it up.

"Put this over your thang," said Zu-Zu, using the wet plastic to keep me from mooning her. She was inventing prophylactics.

Evidence

Once, Zu-Zu crushed a Styrofoam cup and stuck it inside my pants. Zu-Zu got on her knees and begged me to let her feel the cup. But, I was busy drinking a stolen $2 can of Nutrament.

Prayer for Passive Resistance

"Please baby baby please," Zu-Zu whispered. Singing "Don't Be That Way," she glared at Heaven.

For Heaven's Sake

Zu-Zu.

"What's your problem?"

"My blue heaven," Zu-Zu replied.

"Blue heaven is full of coppers," I told Zu-Zu.

"Conception," she said. She kicked Chops' fat chest and stomach and spat in his face.

Tow Away Zone

Zu-Zu flagged a cop and pointed toward Chops. "Come get this fat fucker!"

The cop looked like who-me.

"Yeah, I'm talkin' to you," said Zu-Zu.

The cop glanced at his black lizards to see if he was standing in muddy waters.

"You with the blue uniform."

The whistle dropped out of his mouth.

"You with the big stick and gun on your hip."

He called for help.

"That's right," said Zu-Zu. "Bring your buddies."

The copper came up to Zu-Zu with two other blues. "I've never had a thang blacker than you," he said.

Zu-Zu smacked him in the face. "Wake up, white boy. You stepped out of a dream."

"Pick up your trash, you black dog," said the copper. Just like that. "How would you like to marry Liz behind bars?"

"Don't try to punk me," said Zu-Zu. "Do your job for a change and take this overweight lover to pig heaven."

"What's wrong with him?" asked Charlie Irvine.

"He's dead."

"What happened?"

"He tried to do me."

"No wonder he's dead," said Charlie Irvine. The cops chuckled.

"You're funny," said Zu-Zu, "but your thang is too small to be cracking those kind of jokes." With her index finger and thumb, Zu-Zu showed him about an inch of thin air.

"Take care of the body yourself," said the cop. "The spook can rot there in the earth for all I care. I can't tell this one apart from the dirt and mud anyway (hee, hee)."

"Wait a minute," interrupted another cop. "I think we should bury this chubby nigger . . . to make sure. We've had no more trouble with Martin Luther King since they put him in a coffin."

Chops woke up and gave him the finger. "Forget you," he said. He covered his mouth so the cop couldn't hear him.

After You've Gone

I said, "You've come back as a lemon drop."

Smelly and with bad soil all over him, Chops was sour.

"If someone tries to fade me, I'm going to take them out once and for all," Chops said.

"About that lump on your head, Chops . . . I'm the one who did it. You was out of control."

Chops' eyes went to the back of his head while he rolled around in the mud, trying to get up. "When I get through with you, you gonna wish that you were never out here in this park, you gonna pray for yo' momma and daddy, for a chance to live a normal life."

"Shut up!" I said.

Zu-Zu laughed in his face.

Chops did a circle with his fingers and then pointed to Zu-Zu's skirt. "I'm gonna tear it up," he promised.

Zu-Zu spat in his face. "You done lost your good thang," she said.

Chops was sore as he rubbed the small of his back. He got up on his hands and then fell down again. He put his big hand over his head like it was a black record and scratched it. "I know one thang," he said, "this world is full of spirits."

"Quit talking smack and go to sleep," said Zu-Zu. "Your head has gotta be killing you. And you got no cents to make it worth your while to stay alive."

Chops cleared his throat and groaned. "Monster," he said to me. Minutes later, we heard him snoring.

Confirmation

"What are you?" Zu-Zu asked. "Alien, Hellraiser, the fly,

silence of the lambs, or what? Fess up."

Just as Zu-Zu spat out the words, and The Queen started singing "U-N-I-T-Y" somewhere else in the park, a group of homeless black boys began to peek around us to see if Chops was in fact a dead body.

"I'm Meteor Man, Superfly, too legit to quit," I said. "I couldn't fall in love with a woman, so I left South Central Los Angeles and hitched rides all the way to New York. When I met you at the Metropolitan Museum, I was eating a ketchup sandwich and trying to save myself from the cold, waiting for a train to go through the desert and back to Sunset Boulevard."

"Why is it everything you say sounds like fast food?" Zu Zu asked. She was referring to everything always seemingly being on the surface, that is, having no meaning to the normal Joe Blow or Susie Chapstick who simply couldn't look deep enough to understand people with a different flavor.

I continued talking, smoking dope.

"What's your bag?" Zu-Zu asked.

"You can get if it you really want it," I told Zu-Zu. "But my story goes out mostly to the fellas though. My homies and dumb-ass geez."

"So tell it," Zu-Zu said. "It ain't like you got something else betta' to do." She finally sat down again, her shoe sprawled out in the grass like she was ready to take some notes.

"I am old gangster," I said, loud enough for the musical youth to hear. "When I got to The Big Apple, I was kicking it with Chops' fat-head cousin, Cleetus."

"You mean that big bubble-head skeezy pim-m-m-mp who circles around The Cotton Club on odd weekends?" Zu-Zu asked. She knew Harlem and often compared it to the hair on the back of her neck.

"He still keeps me on a 186," I said, meaning that I was constantly watching for his trifling ass, even though I could never admit it to Chops since Cleetus was his cousin. Where reputation and negritude were concerned, kin stuck together; you never turned yo' back to/on your cousin.

"Why?" Zu-Zu asked. She wanted to know the reason.

"It was a male-bonding thang," I said, checking out the boys who were listening, many of them squatting now, a couple of them looking like they were whispering to others how they could tell that I liked The Dramatics. "You think they [Whitey] care about us?" I asked Zu-Zu. "Not Wall Street. I did drive-bys for the laughs.

"As if caught slanging 40-ounces, and dustin' them, in a black motion picture that we couldn't stop, me and Cleetus lackadaisically walked into a white scene that sold Sta-Sof and other black beauty products. We stood by the front cash register like we were doing a Menace-to-Society, bombs in our big mouths."

Lazily, Zu-Zu crossed her legs and reached for one of the boys' fire before it burned out. "Then what?"

"Talking out of the sides of our necks, we stuck-up the entire store of Asiatic women working for whitey, my wave cap covering the door, Cleetus snatching cigarettes off the nasty shelves and smoking them, the whole nine. While they had their hands up against the wall and their heads turned, Cleetus picked the cotton and floral dress of an older woman and did her until her red flower collapsed, sticking his big head all up in her yellow ass and calling himself 'Curious George' while she was still screaming. Before we moved the crowd, he stopped, set his bottle on the cash register, and spat at the video camera like we was AmeriKKKa's

Most Wanted. After we flew out the door, Cleetus grabbed his thang and waved goodbye, blood all over his pants, his stuppitt brain counting booty and all grossed out, his fingers choking the neck of an empty bottle, 'Bitches' Brew' slipping out of his dirty mouth."

"What if that woman you raped was one of these boys' mothers?" Zu-Zu asked, stretching, instigating. She gave the cigarette back to the boy like it was poison. Everybody went silent and started looking at me real hard.

"Once we got away, I kissed Cleetus bye-bye. 'See ya, and I wouldn't wanna be ya,' I told him. 'We through,' I said. 'I don't want to gang-bang no more.' I gave him the money and told him that I wanted nothing to do with it."

"I definitely can relate," said Zu-Zu, watching the boy puff his own cigarette again and enjoy it. "But it was certainly sissy of you to think that you could just quit doing what you were doing."

"You right, Cleetus cracked up," I said. "He said that I was too late, that I should have thought of that before I got on Candid Camera."

"I bet you didn't even do anything then," said Zu-Zu. I knew from reading her diary that she definitely liked "strong men," brothers who could make a believer out of her. So I tried to appear tough for her, straight like that.

"When Cleetus put some hot buttered soul on his ghetto blaster and sucked on the end of his bomb like he was Teddy Pendergrass, I grabbed him by his shirt which said 'back the fuck up.' After we both did some fancy footwork in the street, I told him to let it go, drop it."

Zu-Zu looked at the penis of the boy with the fire. "I heard that," she said.

"Shut up an' let da man shootdashit!" shouted some teen

from a few yards back treating Zu-Zu like she was my toss-up, apparently while a Nutrament dinner was snaking down his throat.

"Well anyway, 'if the coppers catch us, we dead,' I told Cleetus. He tried to play me off. He called me a splib, then grabbed his dick and gave me the finger."

"Which one?" asked some crank nigga hiding behind the crowd. He was trying to suggest that I was a ho. Zu-Zu grinned, holding the laughter in.

Imagining that I was strapped with a silencer, I pointed my index finger right at the forehead of the brother with the fire, Richie Havens on his tee-shirt staring at me like he had just done Woodstock and wanted to make this affair quick. "Just like you, you trying to rap to my shit in the park, we was always doggin' a nigga out. That was how we was living."

"Man, kiss my ass," he yelled, "I ain't the one who called you out!" He let go of his cigarette and walked away, clutching his crotch area like something was missing.

"Nevermind him, tell the rest of this ghost dance or Folk story or whatever you call this gangster lean," said Zu-Zu, smirking, still pregnant with laughter, trying to hold the baby in as if hoping for an abortion or something.

I hesitated and sent Zu-Zu a heavy "you-got-me-waitin"' look before I continued.

"Anyways, to go on, me and Cleetus shouted at one another until we reached near Rumsey Playfield. We saw a stoned-cold white woman scurry past us with royal blue contacts, water just rolling out of her eyes. While she was trying to run in high heels and a pair of Dazzey Duks, Cleetus whipped her with a coke stare. 'One day you're gonna get it,' I said to Cleetus. 'I sure hope so,' he said. He thought all of this women's violence stuff was funny. He showed me a condom and then threw it away like it was nothing."

"What happened next, Daddy-O?" Zu-Zu asked, her body leaning over to the opposite side now like I was getting stale. "And by the way, I'm not your baby tonight. I'm not your shit, your ho, your bitch, your old lady, or your main squeeze either. Dig-g-g-g?" She spat in my direction.

"Maybe you don't need to know this story," I told Zu-Zu. "Maybe it ain't for you." I turned my back and pretended to be upset.

Suddenly, I did a 180 and came closer to Zu-Zu. "Well, I stopped arguing with Cleetus for a minute and thought about what was really buggin' him: Cleetus had seen a lot of faded boogies. His mama hung herself in Hell's kitchen with a black strap from her own handbag just after his pops was smoked in a car-jacking incident. She had seen everything, including the niggas who did it. She slept in a bathtub until the day she could take it no longer. Cleetus said that she was better off gone anyway because his pops had beaten her so low that she was living on the curb. You know what I'm saying? He played her. Cleetus later finally admitted that he had casually walked into the house and then saw his momma dangling by the counter with ice in her fist.

"When Cleetus saw me clenching white rocks in my hand, he gave me the evil-eye. He must have thought I was his daddy threatening to beat him for carrying a beeper that was useless. 'Go ahead, try me,' he said. I responded, 'The harder they come, the softer they go.'

"'What you do comes back to you,' I told Cleetus."

"Then what happened?" Zu-Zu asked, turning over to the other side one more time, boys and men all around her.

"Yeah, hurry up cause we got ta' go!" someone shouted from the rear of the crowd, fireflies blinking like all this violence stuff was making them sick in the stomach.

"We ain't got all day to be listenin' to some long-ass antique story of pyscho-babble if it don't have that 187 proof," said another nigga, gargling a mouthful of loose juice or Stag or Old E.

I wanted to get him, but, in the dark, the crowd was simply black people with voices.

"Well, to make a long story short, he shot me. The bullet was singing when it tore up my guts, Cleetus running away, his gun giggling. That's when I laid my gun out in the grass."

I looked around at the crowd, most of it eyeing Zu-Zu more than me. "You can get it if you really want it," I said.

"Man, you ain't nothin' but a girl," one of them shouted. Then, like gorillas throwing their feces, they all started hurling clumps of hardened mud at me before they strutted away doing a cock-of-the-walk stride. Only Zu-Zu and Chops remained. Chops was snoring up a storm, his wind growing more disturbed. Zu-Zu eased closer to me and ran her fingers through my afro, massaging my blackest parts.

Lonely Boy

Zu-Zu said, "That's what you are." She grabbed my hand, twisted it, and we fled several yards to a pale blue tent in the park in search of our future.

Sketch 1

There were earrings and cheap gold-electroplated costume jewelry and colored scarves and doo-rags and shreds of mud cloth and Guatemalan worry dolls and poultry and garden snakes all over the ground. On a coffee table sat a Styrofoam cup of black coffee, the color diluted by cream and sugar Zu-Zu squeezed a 60-watt GE lightbulb in a lamp with no shade. A very black woman fixed Zu-Zu good, turning on the light, holding her hand against the bulb, and asking her what she wanted.

"Let go of my hand!" Zu-Zu screamed, the hot bulb burning her skin into a purple plum.

The gypsy woman finally let go. "What's the matter, heifer? You feeling a little hot?"

"What's yo' problem?" Zu-Zu asked. "You want my man?"

"Shut up unless you'd like your tongue cured and a house of starving butch women. Nobody wants what you got. If I wanted a man, I take him. That's how I am, and there's nothing you can do about it. I'm the boss. And I own a doll for every black man in the park. I can put a spell on you in a minute. Make you mine. So shut up, or I'll grab one of your tender loins and give it that whip appeal."

"Enough with that voodoo shit," I said. "We ain't marked for death. If I was Steven Seagal, I would break yo' bones so you could hear the sound of them cracking."

"I would be out for justice then," said the woman, much darker than Zu-Zu.

"It wouldn't make any difference," I said. "I'm hard to kill."

"Maybe," she said, "but I know how to take out the garbage."

"She's wacked, under siege," said Zu-Zu. "Let's blow this joint before we all are attacked by whatever she's got."

"Not so fast, Zu-Zu. If this tramp has got something to say, let her say it."

"I can read you your future, but it's gonna cost you a lot of motherfuckin' money," she said. "You got to pay to play."

"Whore, here's eight dollars and 52 cents," I said. "Make it good."

Gypsy Woman

My black ass. I turned around and looked for a good seat.

"Where are we?" I whispered to Zu-Zu.

"Don't talk, just listen," said Zu-Zu.

"Let me look into my crystal ball," the black woman said. She gazed into the light bulb, the light giving her a headache.

"Damn," she said. "You goin have to wait a while. The spirits are tripping."

"She's higher than all of us," I whispered to Zu-Zu.

"You want your future told or a muzzle on your mouth?" she asked.

"I paid for mumbo-jumbo," I said, wondering just what kind of pyschic friend was she.

"Where did you get the money from anyway?" whispered Zu-Zu.

The black woman ignored us. She shuffled a deck of tarot cards, laid five cards out on the table, and then turned one over picturing a faceless man with an ax on his shoulder.

She screamed. "Fear death by chops!" she said.

Speak No Evil

"Black woman," Zu-Zu warned, "I could kill a nigga for less."

The black woman handed Zu-Zu a leather string of dangling rubbers, signifying the phallus and shit.

"Take this talisman and wear it round yo' neck," she said. "Use it to fight the powers that be."

"You tryin' to be funny or something?" I asked. "You don't care about her."

"Foo', I ain't got to care," she said. "That's yo' job. Now get out of here. I'm tired of looking at you."

Have A Nice Day

Bitch.

Trouble Everywhere I Roam

I looked at Zu-Zu, the talisman around her neck as we

sauntered away.

"Why me?" I asked. I thought about the woman I left behind and the fact that maybe Zu-Zu would never give me love, no matter how nice I was, no matter how much I shied away from the gang-banging.

We strolled below the trees in silence.

Now's The Time

Flukie told Sterling Silver, their raw hands snapping off tiny twigs at the top of an elm tree.

"Shut up," Sterling Silver whispered. "This ain't a concert for cootie. Or coochie. Speak low."

"Let's jump her now," Flukie muttered.

"Be patient," said Sterling Silver. "We will."

In The Small Wee Hours

"We ain't got all day," said Flukie. "If we don't get her, it's our asses."

"It's yo' ass," said Sterling Silver. "You the one that thought up this kidnapping."

"We ain't got to keep our promise."

"There's no way we can hide, nowhere to run," said Sterling Silver. "Not with that Monk-nigga loose."

Sterling Silver tried to look down the inside of Zu-Zu's tube top. "Let's just do it and get it over with," he said.

"The sooner the better," said Flukie, beginning to feel a bit unstable as high as he was.

Sterling Silver finally gave up on seeing the hills of Zu-Zu's titties. "Would you happen to have a Mounds bar?" he softly asked. "I could use some creamy coconut covered with real dark chocolate about now."

"I feel a woody coming on," said Flukie. He and Sterling Silver sat on the heavy branches, emulating dark shadows. No way Zu-Zu could have seen them hovering over her big head like vultures.

Flukie started thinking about his momma. "I ain't no First Blood or Sylvester Stallone, but if they laid a finger on my momma, it's over," he said, fiddling with the red doo-rag on his head so the leaves couldn't destroy out his wave.

Sterling Silver watched Zu-Zu smear Palmer's cocoa butter on the soft spot of her hand where the gypsy had warmed her up. "Word to the muther," said Sterling Silver, recklessly eyeballing Zu-Zu's honey-brown thighs while she bounced, her hips singing "shoop, shoop—shoop, shoop."

Flukie snatched a pointed stick and aimed it at Zu-Zu's brain. "I put a spell on you," he said, the glycerin and activator gel from his doo-rag dropping slowly on Zu-Zu's back.

The Midnight Sun Will Never Set

Now leisurely striding, Zu-Zu started singing "Vampin' Liza Jane," the moon's glow fully cast upon her since it was way after midnight, fog slowly circling around her feet.

"I will cheat death the same way I do a spade in a table top game," Zu-Zu said for kicks.

"You will live forever," I said. We strolled past a capped water fountain, Zu-Zu looking back at it.

"Do you hear laughter?" Zu-Zu asked.

"I hear the trippin' and ailing of the gods being robbed by you and your rogue Queens and kings," I told Zu-Zu.

"Stop patronizing me," she said. She spat in my hair.

"Excuse me, pardon me, don't let me get in your way, Zu-Zu. But if you gonna spit like that, save your breath for a nigga that's worth it."

"Didn't you spit on me?" Zu-Zu asked, rubbing her neck.
"Hell no."

"What's all this shit on my back then?"

"Droppings."

We stopped. Zu-Zu gazed down at the cloud by her feet. "Enough of this Ten Commandments stuff," she said, feeling her heart.

My Funny Valentine

"Kiss me, and I'll kiss you back," I said to Zu-Zu, every Tom, Dick, and Harry in the park listening and trying to get in on the action.

"Let's wait awhile," said Zu-Zu, not interested.

"I want you," I told Zu-Zu just like Marvin Gaye, one of my idols. "And I want you to want me, too."

"What you won't do for love," said Zu-Zu, feeling herself for a pulse.

"Let's get it on," I said.

"Keep on truckin'."

"Distant lover."

"You can't hurry love," said Zu-Zu, trying to see herself in a Sutter Home wine bottle.

"You can't hide love," I said.

"I'm a private dancer," Zu-Zu said, "dancing for money."

"Money can't buy you love."

"Can't buy me happiness either," Zu-Zu added.

"So what do you want it for?"

"Lip surgery, silicone breasts, to have my way."

She silenced me momentarily. I didn't know which way to take her.

"Are you serious?" I asked.

"Do you really want to know?" she responded.

"Baby love," I said. "I got nobody."

Zu-Zu watched as a mosquito bit my neck. "Ain't nobody better," she said.

I slapped the mosquito with one hand, and it dove off the

mane of my neck, doing a full-twisting somersault with about a 3.5 degree of difficulty. It looked up at me from the grass.

"What do you think?" it asked.

"Got to give it up," I said. I put my foot down. "C'mon, Zu-Zu, take one helluva of a chance."

Zu-Zu was not paying attention. She kept looking around, noticing that everybody had suddenly vacated the park.

"What happened to all of the spooks?" Zu-Zu asked.

Ghost Town

"Take anything you want," I said, like this world was mine. We walked over to a trash can and dug up a couple of black western costumes, Zu-Zu furiously throwing everything else to the ground.

"You got a gun?" she asked.

"Yep."

I showed her my nine. She turned and looked the other way like it was nothing.

"You want it?" I asked.

Zu-Zu popped me on the head. "Why would anyone want a gun, nigga?" My knees buckled, Zu-Zu sticking her pretty face between my bowlegs, mumbling "men are such simple creatures.

"Giddy-up," she said.

I got myself back together. "Where are the clowns?" I asked.

"Get up!" Zu-Zu shouted. Her neck was caught between my legs, which fortunately for her were feeling livery that night.

"Gett off!" Zu-Zu shouted, reacting as if she had been on top of a bullock that spun her around to 22 positions.

"Why you sweatin' me?" I asked.

Zu-Zu rolled her head, trying to shake out the cobwebs. "I'm real foggy right now," she said.

I stepped to her smooth and direct. "Yippee-ky-yea," I said. "I'm the fastest gun in the west. Let's just do this with a quickness and get it over with. Let's just do this like bam after a spell of whiskey." I slung my gun around and opened up the cloth cap I was now wearing.

Zu-Zu spat in the dirt. "You must really think you're Superman or Clint Eastwood or hard to kill. You got to have a bigger gun than that to do me. You couldn't shoot Melba Moore with that. Melba toast would have nothing to worry about. You wouldn't have the guts to make holes if a woman gave you a piece of banana nut bread. Even if you knew how to work a gun, yours wouldn't be loaded."

"I can pull the trigger," I said.

"What's wrong? Gun jammed?"

"All it needs is a little lubrication."

"Or, someone to help you hold it."

"Do you mind? I'm beginning to get very hungry."

"Lubricate it yourself," said Zu-Zu, digging deeper into the trash. "Forget the fast food. What I want is a shot of whiskey. The only way you'll do me is if I'm drunk and slobbering over you like a saloon gal."

I drew a bottle of Colt 45 from the trash can with a little booze left in it.

"Check you out," said Zu-Zu. "You like Mr. GQ Smooth now."

"Yep," I said, the industrial spurs spinning on my black dingo boots like throwing stars mowing the grass.

"Don't touch me," said Zu-Zu, staring at my spurs like they were wheels of fortune, the best thing for a homeless person since gravy.

59

"Shut up, Zu-Zu. This ain't Dodge City, and you ain't Kitty. But even if the clearing fog was gunsmoke, we'd still be in trouble cause Harlem is like Tombstone. Saddle up so we can split this ghost town. I feel like Doc Holliday just before he got faded."

"John Wayne," said Zu-Zu, "you've come back to me."

"What the hell you talkin' bout?"

Zu-Zu pointed at a badly-etched inscription on the handle of my gaat [gun]. "Why Johnny, you can't read."

I waved goodbye with one hand.

"Five-card stud," Zu-Zu said.

"Five fingers of death," I replied. Every nigga in the hood admired the quickness, strength, and power of Bruce Lee.

Zu-Zu started shouting: "Johnny's got a gun, and is goin' to cap a woman. A 29-year old Butch Cassidy with a nine he found in the trash. He's a cowboy who'd rather rope cattle and catch dogies in a pair of rawhide boots than kill for a pair of Cons."

I did a few tricks with my gun and pointed at Zu-Zu's booty. "Out here, everybody got a piece," I shouted.

Warm Valley

"A little closer," begged Sterling Silver, waiting patiently in the tree until he could look straight down into Zu-Zu's top.

Tallest Trees

They started talking smack. "Why is it the tallest trees are climbed by the littlest niggas?" they asked themselves.

"Shut the you-know-what up," said Flukie.

The mad tree dropped Sterling Silver and Flukie in the dirt, right on their funky booties, their bodies rolling through the mud and wet land until they crashed into my boots and stopped, their faces stuck on my toes like black olives poked by toothpicks.

Zu-Zu cheesed, American style, processed. "Howdy, boys," she said.

"Who are these guys?" I asked Zu-Zu, figuring she had to know them.

"Guess," said Flukie.

"Gucci," said Zu-Zu.

"No, I mean guess who we are," said Flukie.

"Humpty Dumpty," said Zu-Zu.

"Amos and Andy," I said.

"D.J. Jazzy Jeff and Fresh Prince," said Zu-Zu.

"Eddie Murphy and Arsenio Hall," I said.

"Chuck D and Flavor Flav," said Zu-Zu.

"What are you, stupid?" asked Sterling Silver.

"Give you a hint," said Flukie. "We mean, vileness."

"He means 'we villains,'" said Sterling Silver.

"Batman and Robin," said Zu-Zu.

"Beevus and Butthead," I said. I had peeped them one day on a billboard.

"Just shut up," said Sterling Silver. "This ain't *Jeopardy* or *Name That Tune.*"

"Whatever happened to *Name That Tune*?—that was the one show I liked as a little kid," Zu-Zu whispered.

Flukie stood up and waved his gun at my mouth. "I wouldn't talk back to him if I were you," Sterling Silver said. "He's got a trigger-finger and hates it."

"What do you boys want?" Zu-Zu asked.

Sterling Silver would not talk to her. "Give us the girl, Bronco Billy, or your balls are in double jeopardy."

"Don't do anything nutty, Wesley Hardin," said Flukie, imitating. "This is a $400 gaat sold to us from Whitey. It can blow your head clean off with one shot. If you don't believe the hype, go head and make my day, Billy Boy."

"But remember that even a yellow nigga like you can be faded," Sterling Silver added.

"Step off," said Zu-Zu. "Every dog has his day."

"Stop that cow from chewing," Sterling Silver told Flukie. "She got a mouth bigger than The Queen of Soul, but sounds like Aunt Jemima."

Zu-Zu looked shamed and insulted. "Take care of 'em for me, Johnny," she said.

"Stop calling me 'Johnny'!"

"Alright, you yellow Billy The Kid, it's your show," said Sterling Silver. "Quit baitin' with your banana and all that mushy talk. Are you gone give us the girl, or do we have to take her?"

"Where you want this cap, homey?" Flukie asked. "This gun is gettin' awfully itchy."

Sterling Silver peeped at Flukie. "You don't look like you got nothin'," he whispered.

"I ain't studdin' you," Flukie said. "I tell you what. I betcha' I know the number of times I had my dick sucked."

Zu-Zu spat in his face. "You're disgusting."

"Yep," said Sterling Silver. "Now let's get on with the show."

"You bad," I said. "Go ahead. Make your move."

"Bad," said Flukie. "Three sounds. B-A-D."

"Shut up, Flukie," said Sterling Silver. "I don't care if you are hooked on phonics. This ain't Romper Room."

"Damn—whatever happened to *Romper Room*?" Zu-Zu whispered. "That was a great show."

"This ho thinks she's in Kansas with her dog Toto," said Sterling Silver. "I can't wait to do her."

Flukie rushed closer and grabbed Zu-Zu's tit, grinning from ear to ear.

"You so ugly you scared all the crows away," Zu-Zu said.

The tallest trees kneeled and said a prayer for Zu-Zu.

Take The "A" Train

Flukie grabbed his crotch and stood in Zu-Zu's face. "Oh, so you a lively-bitch," he said. "How would you like to come service me? I'll whip that ass into shape. Consider the goose pimples on your cheeks as grits."

Sterling Silver chuckled. "Look, Flukie. She can let it go, and, like dust, that rickety booty is gone with the wind. Chee, chee."

"Enough talk," I said. "Draw."

Flukie searched his baggy pants for a pen or pencil or etch-a-sketch.

"Shoot," Sterling Silver shouted. "Finish this kindergarten cop before I get mad and blow away Monk's girl."

"Draw," I said.

"Smoke him," said Sterling Silver.

"Draw," I said.

"I got no papers!" Flukie cried.

Sterling Silver sent Flukie a mean stare, like for crack-heads. "What are you, cainin' or something? Take that boy out and smoke him!"

"See ya," said Zu-Zu. She gave me that cheek-to-cheek comfort and then moved the crowd.

We stood silent in a triangle, each man beginning to draw border lines with their feet.

Theme From The Good, The Bad And The Ugly

It was early in the morning, the cocks crowing. Sleepy, we squinted at one another, our hands covering our guns, trying to get a feel for where the cocks were.

"This feels good," said Flukie, the zipper open in his baggies, his big head surrounded by the blowing hairs of a tree's armpit.

"What's up with all this black?" said Sterling Silver, pointing his index finger at me as if it were directing a shitload of mean bullets.

"There's little or no light for us," I said. "Plus, we're soiled and dirty. And, gaats are evil. So why don't we just stop the violence and pray for peace in the barrio or burrough or whatever you want to call this shoot-'em-up place?"

"I got your piece," said Sterling Silver, the fingers on his right hand doing the Harlem shuffle toward his gun.

"It's the ho we want," said Flukie. "Give us the ho and we outta here lickety-split."

"With a quickness," Sterling Silver added in. "Otherwise, you'll get a taste of these nasty silver bullets."

They took a few more steps back. I spread my cape and showed them my holster, running my grungy fingers over the encased bullets as if they were a line of condoms. "Shoot," I said.

Sterling Silver looked to the side. Flukie rocked back and forth, his hands sweating. "Let's go," he said.

"Why you sweating me?" Sterling Silver asked. It was times like these that made him wonder why he had quit working the kitchens to hang out in the ghetto with a loco nigga who never had his back. "Nevermind," he said. "I don't even want to know."

"No more talk," I said.

The theme music played as we backed up even more, our legs apart. Flukie started checking out me and Sterling Silver, whose own trigger-finger was now twitching. Flukie felt the tension and pressure sticking him like dirty needles, once again getting him high, infecting him with a deadly virus that, like a retaliating gang of spooks, would certainly haunt him one day. Flukie was a dead man. He felt on his penis some more to stay hard and cool.

"When the music stops, you niggas will die hard," I said.

The theme music played. Sterling Silver angled his black body where I could barely see him, perhaps shadowing thangs to come, his big lips singing a mix of Michael Jackson's "Bad" and "Smooth Criminal," his figure shaded by the trees, his right leg crooked, his brown belt sportin' a tarnished silver buckle, his hardened hards moving the buckle, his beady hair cut into a V at the back, angry red bumps clustered around his neckline, most of his teeth capped or rotten. He stared around for Kansas and a black hat. When he couldn't find a hat, he pulled a bent silver baby spoon out of his shirt pocket and stuck it in his mouth.

"When the music stops, hasta la vista, babies."

As the music played, it finally hit me what I was getting myself into: Real blood. Real weapons. Real death. I put a bubble gum cigar in my mouth and chewed on it, quickly working my way down to the butt. Flukie took off his doo-rag and used it to wipe his face, Sta-Sof beginning to roll down the side. He wrung the rag for several seconds and then put it back on his head. I didn't draw then because I didn't want the blues to bury the nigga without his wave cap.

Flukie seemed grateful. "Watch where you shoot those silver bullets," he told Sterling.

"Die, you dogs!" Zu-Zu shouted from somewhere unknown to man.

Flukie glanced behind himself to see if there was a cemetery there, a grave ready to put a nigga six-feet under, a tombstone marked "unknown."

"What's the hottie's name?" he asked, still searching for Zu-Zu.

I picked up what proved to be for them a piece of fool's gold or something and pretended to write on it with a crayon while their eyes got big. Then I threw the rock back down and opened my cape a bit more, the butt almost gone between my lips, my eyes partly closed, the musical chimes beginning to slow down, Flukie staring down at the rock like he thought it would make him rich, Sterling Silver covering his precious buckle and pretending to be Ready For The World singing "let's get straight down to business."

Day-Breaking Blues

A fine-ass woman walked by tripping. "Can't we have one day where there ain't no fighting?"

Spur of the Moment

"Thang," said Zu-Zu. She was jealous. She saw the woman checking me out.

Peace

"I'm outta here," the woman said. "I got two kids and nobody at home right now to watch them."

So What

"Nobody asked for your two cents anyway," said Zu-Zu.

Black, Brown and Beige

As the chimes winded down, we edged closer to grabbing our guns—Sterling Silver's face pitch black, Flukie staring at the rock, his stomach withdrawing and wishing the rock was cocaine, Zu-Zu shouting that a gunfight would kill a light-skin nigga like me.

That's what I liked about Zu-Zu. She was always looking out for me.

"It's over," said Zu-Zu. "You don't stand a chance."

"Be optimistic," I said. The line was from The Sounds of Blackness.

"I like their concept!" Zu-Zu shouted. "Very positive! They

got some strong black men and women!"

"Yep," I said. I spat out a chaw of gum and let it hit my dingo boots. I wished that it had been baseball or basketball card gum instead. It cost more, but the cigars were always stale.

"Hubba-Bubba," said Zu-Zu, "it looks like this is your last dance. I hear footsteps, niggas scattin'. It's all bop to me."

"Boplicity," I said. "These niggas ain't shit. The situation looks deeper than what it really is. It takes two to tango. Don't make me over. Me and you got more bounce to the ounce. I can jam. When the popping starts, yoyo get funky."

I threw Zu-Zu a weak shovel, the body all broke-down.

"You talking to me?" Zu-zu asked, acting like she was Yoruba. Flukie pulled his hand out of his pants.

"Yep."

"I don't think so," said Zu-Zu. "Your sugar is gone. One minute, you're nicey-nicey. The next minute, you're just like all the other men."

"Shut up, bitch!" said Flukie.

Sterling Silver cracked up, breaking up into pieces, the spoon going shake-shake-shake in his mouth, his cheeks stretched out like he was the Joker. "Tell me," he said, his whole figure a dusty rose, "have you ever danced with the devil in the pale moonlight?"

Here was a man who gave up being brown and beige. Darn that dream. Black was all he ever wanted to be. Koko. Hot chocolate. Body and soul, the mouse and the man.

Rudy A Message To You

"Two sevens clash," I said. "Things come to bump. You can even be Prince of Darkness if you want, but if you can live, if you can live, if you can live . . . pray for me, man, and for a beautiful day in the neighborhood."

Silent Prayer

Sterling Silver refused to say anything else aloud. Flukie's fingers started twitching. Zu-Zu sang "Trouble in Mind Blues." I opened my cape further, the gun and light holster slinging up-and-down my hip. With the wind gusting—my pants flaring out, I could smell Flukie's Brut cologne and funky attitude, the perspiration rolling down the side of his chest, the small holes in his arm taking it all in, laughing. Flukie could feel himself wet and his gun withdraw; he reached down and pushed it forward. The showdown was supposed to be the climax. Zu-Zu ducked and hid. I spat again, as if to dedicate this fight to her. Zu-Zu wanted nothing to do with it. She gave me the finger, then began to polish her nails. Sterling Silver continued cracking up, his gun shaking all over the place. Flukie couldn't take it. He drew his weapon. I drew my gun and fired what felt like an endless train of shots. I heard bullets cussing and fussing and discussing who to fuck up as they went everywhere. In hair, through bottles, past children. Adult niggas started crying and dying and falling to the ground like shredded leaves or shredded wheat. Zu-Zu crawled into the brush and fell out, the talisman barely able to hang on to her little neck. The trees leaned over to get out of the way of stray bullets, pissed-off and misdirected like juvenile delinquents. Pandemonium erupted. Ashy niggas and dusties went everywhere, forgetting about looking dap. Hot shells played pepper with winged maxi pads and fried chicken legs, a lot of innocent bystanders dropping blood. Sterling Silver's gun licked his lips like Colonel Sanders taking part in Custer's last stand. I saw pickle spears and spears made of tree branches being hurled at my feet. While everyone, including homeless women, were doing "the running man," Flukie darted over to the brush, tore the talisman off Zu-Zu's neck, and dragged her pretty head away. I wasn't a killer, but, out of fear, I kept trading bullets with Sterling Silver like they were Crane potato chip basketball cards going out-of-style. Kareem. He was the cream of the crop. He was a playground legend from Power, but Magic would undoubtedly end up being the collector's item in the barrio; it seemed niggas had to have it to survive the gang-bangin' and frightening levels of hatred. Zu-Zu screamed for help, but no one stopped to listen. She clung to a condom while Flukie shredded her blouse, Zu-Zu reaching back for anything she could grab and hold on to. She uprooted small trees and plants, creating a trail of disturbed greenery and murdered African violets. With his gun out of bullets, Flukie slapped Zu-Zu's breasts like they were pints of bad chocolate milk. He even yawned upon realizing that her nipples were no better or bigger than a dirty penny. She stuck a root in his mouth. He chewed it until rootbeer dripped out. I aimed my gun at Flukie and tried to smoke him, but I ran out of bullets; they were out in the distant field playing hide-and-seek, blood having gotten on their nerves. Sterling Silver cracked up. He thought it was funny. He kissed my bullets goodbye as they crawled under rocks and park benches, and into people's dark clothing. Sterling Silver's soiled skin looked like an earthquake had hit it. Temperamentally, he shot at my head. I kneeled down and begged for forgiveness.

"Pardon me," I said. "My behavior was inexcusable. I was neglected as a child, so I never learned to respect others."

Zu-Zu was still screaming.

"Hi, ho...take her away!" Sterling Silver shouted. Flukie smacked her, then dragged her off, Zu-Zu's face bleeding 86¢ lipstick.

"God," I said. "You are the man. Help me."

Sterling Silver squeezed harder on his gun. "You think I was born with a silver spoon in my mouth?" he asked. "What makes you think God is a he? He could be a she, and the world coming to an end could be five days of bleeding, Her period.

"After all, if God was a man, why would he let us fight and kill one another like this?"

"The Lawd works in strange ways," I said. "But probably not the way you see it."

"Where I come from, it's all good," said Sterling Silver. "We the ones smokin' one another. It's called survival. It's a jungle sometimes, but what else have we got to do?"

He walked up and pushed me in the chest. "Get with the program," he said.

"Don't push me," I said, "cause homes are always provisional. I hate for you to find out the hard way, say six feet under."

Sterling Silver pressed his gun against my big lips and fired.
You're Nicked

He cracked up. I fell into a momentary trance, blood bobsledding down my cold chin tripping and shit about how white I looked when Sterling Silver cocked the gun.

"Jesus!"

He stuck the gun inside my mouth and ordered me to suck on it.

"Chist!"

He kicked me in the crotch, put his finger on the cock, and uttered "pop go da weasel."

I heard one shot. I closed my eyes and thought "adios, Amigo" or "how the west was won" or "unforgiven." When I opened them, I saw Sterling Silver sprinting away, busting out. Even his gun was laughing, smoke coming out of its mouth.

I stayed on my knees until I finished my prayer. "Thank you, God," I said. "But if you were really a woman, you would have taken that gun away from him, wouldn't you?"

As I watched Sterling Silver slither away, I thought about something Zu-Zu once said: "The three evils of the world that a woman can suffer are to live in another's house, to beg, and to be a pauper. But, a man who does evils, expects evil."

Spit In The Sky and It Fall In Your Eye

That was what was to be learned out of all of this madness. I chilled on a bench in Central Park and flashed back to the time Zu-Zu and I snuck through the back door of a jazz set, bogarted our way through a waiting line at the bar, sat down at a reserved non-smoking table, and had candlelight dinner with white wine. Later the same evening, Zu-Zu had black velvet and said that she never felt so good.

When we left the club, Zu-Zu stole the China plate for a souvenir. I swiped two cloth napkins, a wine glass, the incense burner, and a long black candle.

"Put the candle back," Zu-Zu said when we got up from the skirted table.

"What for?"

That was vintage Zu-Zu. She was forever sensitive. She dedicated her life to discussing cheap "tricks" and the fact they sell for money. She was always stealing off somebody, and resisting giving back. Chops once said that the only way he could ever get Zu-Zu was if he whittled her down.

Blues Inside and Out

Zu-Zu was 100% woman.

I lowered my head in Central Park and sung "Heart-Breaking Blues," now that she was gone.

East of the Sun

Where nobody cared, Zu-Zu had kissed and run. She was

probably in the streets of Harlem, being pulled through the crowds as if the city was Bangladesh or Ghana, a hell for the homeless. She was probably singing.

Improvisation

"Where you taking me!"

"Just keep on walkin'," Flukie said to Zu-Zu.

"What we had was good," Zu-Zu said. She was thinking of when she was with me.

Improvisation

People passing stop and stare at me in the park. Then they slide on, buzzing about the rumor that Mister Magic might play in New York.

"Bring back the days of Grover Washington Jr.," I tell them.

"We're talking about Magic Johnson, Mister."

Improvisation

"There's fifty bucks in it for you if you just cooperate," Sterling Silver told Zu-Zu, dragging her through bushes.

"Money can't buy you love, can't buy you happiness," Zu-Zu replied. "The best things in life are free." Zu-Zu was doing some serious trash-talking, making everything up as they inched onward.

Improvisation

Changes

"Whatever you want," Zu-Zu said. Flukie has got his gun inside her skirt.

"Shut up unless you want to get a shot in the ass." He tightly squeezed her arm and entangled his legs around hers.

Improvisation

Unexpected twist.

Chops came running up out of nowhere and said that it was up to us now to get Zu-Zu back.

Hold On

"To your love," I said to myself. I dedicated my life and my next move to Zu-Zu. Then I grabbed Chops and moved the crowd, Chops shouting, proclaiming that we were Batman and Robin in Gotham City.

"Somebody phone the commissioner's office or immigration department," I heard some crank say.

If You're Not Part of the Solution, You're Part of the Problem

I had to check that buster.

Easy Does It

Zu-Zu was getting a little annoyed with the way Flukie was handling her. She pulled away and showed him her tits and ass.

"Dickie's dream," she said.

"Lady be good," said Sterling Silver.

"She ain't nothing but ham n' eggs," said Flukie.

"I am what I am," Zu-Zu said. She sounded like Gloria Gaynor or Gloria Steinem singing "I will survive."

They finally reached Monk at Rumsey Playfield, and he checked her out closely like he was into the black market or something.

"I want a little girl," he said.

"Swell," said Zu-Zu. "I'm about to be raped by Lester Young."

He slapped her, and she spat in his sorry face.

He pushed her down to the ground. "Since you like using yo' mouth so much, why don't you try this?" He unzipped his pants and showed her his gun.

"You must be kidding," Zu-Zu said. "That thing is so old; if you ask me, it's a civil war piece."

Monk did a moten swing but missed her. "You lucky," he

said. "Usually I don't miss."

Monk whistled through his fingers to summon his boys. Then he sat and waited. He tried to make the mind and body one like Buddha.

Four and More

Monk's posse rushed in, carrying sawed-off guns and poker cards, and fixed themselves around Zu-Zu. They roped her and gagged her mouth with a dirty bandanna.

"Suck me until I tell you to stop," the bandanna told Zu-Zu. She sang a lonesome lullaby, hoping that Monk would go ahead and doze off since he was trying to reach the spirit world anyway.

Monk opened his eyes. "That's not the kind of spirit world I'm trying to reach," he said. He asked his boys if they hit the drugstore like he told them. They broke out with ten cans of Nutrament and a carton of cigarettes. Monk did a sugary grin, then swung at the long ponytail of one of his boys.

"Boss, you missed," said another one of his boys.

"So I did," said Monk. "You got a problem?"

Ben Hodges sneaked away, holding his head to get himself back together.

Rubber Neck

Racing through the park, me and Chops felt our heads wobbling as if they were on necks made of latex.

"You think we'll ever find her?" Chops asked.

"Be optimistic," I said. I couldn't help but wonder where Chops had been all this time.

Chops couldn't run for long. He stopped to listen to a fat lady singing. "It's over," Chops said. "We're too late."

"Shut up and run!" I shouted.

"I'm dead," Chops said.

I snatched his big head and tossed it forward. "Run."

Chops sighed. "I'm tired of running," he said. "You go ahead."

I called him a "rudie." Then I moved the crowd without him. But 30 seconds later, Chops called me back. "Wait a minute," he said. "Just give me a moment to tuck in my tee-shirt."

Meanwhile, Back at the Ranch

Monk and the boys sat around and played poker like they were waiting for Loop Garoo Kid to ride in from Yellow Back Radio Broke-Down. As legend and they tell it, the infamous Loop was a bullwhacker so arrogant and unfeeling that he would stamp "ship to Thailand" on the rears of virgin woman, demand their coin for postage, and send them to whore houses without protection.

Loop may have been an icon for Monk, but to Zu-Zu he was an anti-hero. "Why don't you just get on with it?" she asked.

They readied themselves like players in a jazz set, home on the range: Monk poked out his lips to play alto sax. Flukie was on the serpent, his hands inside his pants. Sterling Silver on bass, booming in Zu-Zu's face while talking yin-yang (Chinese principles of good and bad which he borrowed from Confucius and Monk). Ranch-hand Arthur Walker on dumb-piano, standing silent behind the rest of the posse. The real black cowboy, Bill Pickett, on guitar, plucking strands of Zu-Zu's hair, his doggie Spradley eating dry Tang nearby. Cattle rustler Isom Dart did drums, musical glasses, nose-flute, Moog synthesizer, small-pipes, bazooka and glass harmonica. He tried repeatedly to go straight but was unable to give up his addiction to trying anything. Hodges got on the horn, talking fast between baby breaths and clutching his long rifle. Nat Love, better known as "Deadwood Dick," liked virginals but agreed to take a mouth organ.

Zu-Zu sat tied up like Mary Fields, a.k.a. Stagecoach Mary. She clenched her hands, making them shake bad like fists of fury.

The men all paused. They knew that they were looking good. They were holding on to their guns. Their hair was fierce. They saw themselves riding in Zu-Zu's coach like it was an easy rental Ryder.

Pickett restarted the action by snatching crumbs of stolen Revlon and caked-on makeup off Zu-Zu's face.

"Leave it on!" Love demanded. "The more makeup and mascara, the merrier."

Hodges called Zu-Zu "painted woman," thinking he was fly. It wasn't clever or even ornery, but the name stuck among the posse.

Zu-Zu spat in their faces. Monk walked over and swung at her.

"Boss, you missed," said Dart.

"Tough cookie," said Monk, thinking of Mrs. Fields.

Love's lips were bleeding. He dashed for a washcloth, blood falling to the ground.

"You popped him good," Walker said softly.

Monk threw a can of beer and spat in Zu-Zu's face. "He'll be back."

The men all paused like they didn't know if he would come back. Meantime, Monk realized that Zu-Zu had managed to spit and talk and sing with her big mouth gagged. He was pissed.

"Who put that weak bandanna over her mouth?" Monk asked. He untied the knot and threw the thing away.

"Give it back to me!" Zu-Zu shouted. "It's dirty, but it's cotton—and I like cotton."

The bandanna cried tears of joy. "Look at me," it said. "Did you see the way she sucked me? I'm all wet, and she wants me back. I don't know what to say."

Zu-Zu cut loose from the ropes. "I'm free!" she shouted. "I'm free!"

"Silence!" said Monk. He stepped over and shoved the cotton in her mouth. "If you want the bandanna, you can have it. I'm gonna take what's mine. Wipe the makeup off your face."

"No!" Love screamed, running back to the gang. "She's a woman. Love her the way she is, or leave her and let another man dominate her."

Monk stretched his long face and experienced a flashback of his teacher, who was left in a smalltime, depressed Illinois community (POP. 94,583) still gang-bangin' on the east side. Still dealin' in Longview, near Center Street and Hood's BBQ on Martin Luther King Boulevard, where the city had closed off six roads to drive-thru traffic as if the pestilence, the black plague, had to stay there forever.

"Why the shaved head?" Monk asked, coughing a bit.

His teacher tossed a hair brush with genuine boar bristles into the front entrance of a crack house. Like Monk, he never knew his real daddy.

"Cause that's how I show my love for the family," said teacher. "Grand Street Disciples. Peace." He poured beer on the sidewalk, which had been bombed with fat caps, blue paint and Stag and red blood splashed everywhere, puddles filling up the holes.

"What if I don't wanna go out like that?" Monk asked.

"You either get free money or disappear while you can," said Teacher. "It's like that, and that's the way it is." He flashed some signs and offered Monk another swig of alcohol. "What's the matter, nigga? Can't you take your liquor? I don't wanna hear all that coughin' and shit. Dat shit's for babies."

"My momma says what we doin' is wrong," Monk said, stepping back. "She says children are like clay; it all depends on whose hands they're put in."

"The goal of initiation into a gang is submission!" shouted Teacher. "If you cain't be tough, then you got to go!"

Monk kneeled by Teacher's sandals. "Yes, Teacher. I beg forgiveness. I kissed the very ground you walk on. Please, show me love. And I will do what you want me to do."

As Teacher went to hug him, Monk snatched the gaat that was halfway tucked inside the front of Teacher's pants and aimed at his big head.

Teacher took a swig of Stag, close enough for Monk to smell his bad breath and feel the spit coming out of his mouth. "Go head," he said. "Squeeze that shit, you black pussy. Or are you just going to keep standin' dere, posin' like a Siamese cat without a tin roof to play on?"

"Why you make me do dis?" Monk asked. "When I started doin' stuff at school for you, I didn't know what I was doin'."

"And you still don't," said Teacher. He grabbed the gun and ripped it out of Monk's hand. "This ain't 'Kung Foo'. You ask too many damn questions. If my daddy never spanked me, what makes you think you can?" In anger, Teacher threw down his beer bottle, shattered glass dealing in dirt.

Monk grabbed a thick piece of glass and waved the sharp edges. "I'm not like you," he said. "I ain't no murderer. I wanna jet. And only you can let me go."

"Okay, okay, okay," said Teacher, "if it's dat deep fo' you. But I never want to see yo' ugly face again."

Monk turned around and started kicking, scared of being beaten and run-in by Five-O, and knowing that Teacher would eventually change his mind.

Teacher stepped over the red body that was on a section of the graffiti. Even though he had been shot three times, including once in the head, the black male was still crawling a few inches down the walk, his fingers extended. "Grand Street Disciples, nigga!" said Teacher. Then he kicked the teenager and flew, laughing aloud, thinking of how funny the boy looked when he put his gun in Monk's hand and told him to "squeeze that shit."

Meantime, Monk was sprinting alongside a railroad track and in sewage, wondering if he would smell by the time he got to Harlem and tried to fit in as a migrant.

Show Me the Way to Go Home

Walker wanted nothing to do with what he thought was going to be a cosmetic make-over.

"Follow the travelin' light to Forty Second Street," Monk said, slowly squeezing an empty can of beer. When Walker turned his back, Monk dropped the can and swung at him.

"Boss, you missed," said Love.

"It ain't no thing," said Monk. But, Dart was holding his crotch in pain. "What you hit me for?"

"I never liked you anyway," Monk said. "You remind me of a nigga from the projects. Now shut up and tie her up real good. She's deliberately trying to skip the torment. She's spitting in our faces to make us wanna kill her."

The posse stared at one another. "Did you give him the right pack of cigarettes?" Love asked Pickett.

"I gave him Kool," Pickett said.

"Then why ain't he satisfied with the slow motion?" Dart asked.

"What is this?" Monk asked. "A meeting in the ladies room? Hurry up and rope her before she gets loose! Brand her government inspected, then let's move the crowd and herd

79

some more young pretty girls before the other gangs corner the black market!"

Sterling Silver ordered Flukie not to budge. "Our money first!" Sterling Silver insisted.

"I don't owe you nothing!" said Monk. "Get going before you get hurt!"

"I'm going home to momma," said Flukie. He took off.

"Look at that spook go!" The boys all laughed heartily. Monk busted up.

"We'll be back," Sterling Silver promised. He turned and chased after Flukie, Spradley barking and chasing after both of them for fun.

"Let's get out of here before those lugheads come back," Monk said. "Hide the girl behind the telephone pole or tall trees lined up there. She should feel at home with all those dicks standing in line."

Monk liked hangin' with the homeboys from the set because they always laughed at his joke.

Fee Fi Fo Fum

Monk enjoyed being a giant. He strutted towards nirvana.

Giant Steps

Making impressions. Monk improvised his ascension. He was live at the Village Vanguard. He was Soultrane. Meditations. Africa/Brass. "One of my favorite things," said Love, "Supreme."

Monk climbed a steep hill, yelling for the new DJ, Shep Pettibone, to remix his life. On what was becoming just another partly sunny but hazy day in the hood, Pettibone started scratching Blue Magic and "(I'm a) Dreamer" into Smoke City's "Dreams" and "(We're Living) In The World of Fantasy." That's how bad he was. The nigga could cut-up. He was like C & C Music Factory. He could jam on vinyl like

Michael Jackson or Guy. With a drink in his hand, he could take four Gemini 1200 turntables and mix them all at once, without using slip discs or scratch pads. He frequently did Island mixes, like DJ Kool Herc fresh from Jamaica. And if you couldn't understand his concept, he'd do toasting and tell you point blank, "It ain't fo' you."

"Let's go," Monk said. He wanted to see his boy spin. Off in the distance, Shep sounded like he had broke out with a bottle of alcohol in each hand and was splashing together rhythms for a megamix...

Living In The Bottle

Sloshing alcohol over the tables proved to be Shep's calling card. With probably two cross-faders and an echo control, he mixed extended versions of "Pray" and "Like A Prayer" with "Erotic City" and "Feels Good." Me and Chops could hear him scratching the black grooves, not missing on anything.

Just A Touch Of Love

"All I want to do before we leave is feel her, see where's she's been," said Nat Love.

All Around The World

"Why don't we just give up?" Chops asked. He had something else in mind, but I could tell he was keeping it a secret.

No One's Gonna Love You

Zu-Zu spat in Love's face. "I'm just sittin' away, gettin' lonely," she said.

Heavily strapped, Pickett slogged over to her and slumped. "When did you first spit on a nigga?" he asked. "Do you remember the time?"

"Send me forget-me-nots," said Zu-Zu, "to help me to remember."

Pump It

A brother cheered as we raced past him, Chops producing bite-size Snickers and beginning to die.

U Can't Touch This

Zu-Zu spat in Pickett's face. "To Sir with Love," she said.

Control

"I need her alive, and kicking," said Monk.

Can't Stop

I told Chops, "Forget about your chocolate-covered peanuts." We stared at an old "dog" dressed in drag and trying to turn tricks out on the street. "I'm looking at you, you're looking at me," I said to the man, who I had seen staring at me many times before in the cheese line.

He chuckled. "I'm walking down the street watching ladies go by, watching you."

"Keep on walkin' then," I said while Chops was singing "I See Love."

"Time out," said Chops, like he was trying to sit down a kid.

"This is no ordinary love," I said. I broke out with some hip-hop. Chops must have felt that he had no choice but to follow.

Observers tried to jump bad, asking us why we was running so goofy.

"I got ants in my pants," I replied. I stopped and shook 'em out. About eight greedy little niggas and an albino cockroach dropped out of my drawers. Three of them still had food and Nutrament in their mouths; their jaws were tight.

"Can't you see we're trying to party?" they asked. "What's yo' problem?"

An ant who seemed immune to the Raid stuff let go of the barbecue pork in his mouth and looked up at me, tripping. "Look, My Brother, I hate to break it to you, but this ain't

Beale Street," he said. "Get yo' program together. Dig?"

I smashed the ant with my foot and crushed his black ribs. He flagged me and then died, but not before a joint came out of his mouth.

"This ain't *Hill Street Blues* either," I said. "Move the crowd. And take your roaches with you."

"We don't need a crowd to have a party," another ant said. He was dragging a roach like it was nothing, the dope making him stagger.

I put my foot in his ass. "You're buggin' out," I said. I shook my foot, but he wouldn't get off.

"Gett off!" I shouted.

"When doves cry," the bug said. His booty was hanging out, and, like a trained army ant, he attempted to fall into the trenches in the sole of my muddy boot. I rubbed him off with the spur of my other boot.

The ant pulled out Flash photos of me and ripped them like he was Sinead O'Connor. "You've got a split personality, Sybil," he said.

"Don't make me over," I told the black ant. Then I finished him in front of Chops standing there. Witnessing the whole thing, he was breathing badly with melted nougat running down his chin.

The last ant started backing up; 187 proof was all he needed. With a little alchohol squirting through his big lips, he stuck his middle finger in a glass bottle with a brown paper bag around it. "That's yo' momma!" he said. Obviously, he and his band had decided to go down like Prince and the Revolution.

"Good night, sweet Prince," I said, "now cracks a noble heart." I stepped on him and kept going, blood all over my big toe.

He flipped over several times before landing on his side. "Te quiero," he said, his fingers begging me to come on, but his other arm crushed underneath his body.

I did the Spanish hustle trying to get away from this wild gang of ants, probably from Sugar Hill. Chops fled with me, protecting his candy bars.

"You go boy!" shouted a black boy clinging to a can of Nutrament and an almost empty bottle of coke.

I turned around and blew dust in his face like it was clouds from God's feet and like I was Michael Jackson dancing, doing a Pepsi commercial.

"Beat it," I told him.

"Don't even think about it," he said. "My name is Calvin. You know, Calvin from the corner. I know you know me. I work at McDonalds part time to please my mother, but I deal drugs and bootlegged wax at school to make real money. Soon, I'll be managing my own store, sellin' dope beats, dope rhymes, dope cuts. I'll be yo' pusher." He flashed a couple of folded hundred dollar bills. "May I take yo' order?"

"What would the white people in Head Start say if they could see you now?" I asked.

"They'd say that I had too much apple pie."

"The American Dream might be nasty sometimes, but it works," said Chops, eyeing the boy to check if he had any McDonalds food on him, a fat burger or fun meal.

"Don't encourage him," I told Chops. "We've got enough mad characters out on the street already. We need to stay positive, upbeat."

The boy pointed at a long line of colored women soliciting near the clusters of sidewalk talk. "Wild women don't worry, wild women don't get the blues," he said.

"Shut up!" I told the kid. "This ain't Africana or women's

studies. Take yo' little black ass home."

The boy showed me two keys, including one for valet parking at Small's nightclub and resturant, and shook them, fish on his breath. "I got a mixed lady who drives a black Maxima in a black neighborhood."

"I hope you doing safe sex."

"Got to go get ready," he said. Next thing we knew, he ran like eyeliner, his big feet leaving black streaks and dark shadows on the pavement where his high-class basketball shoes had rubbed it the wrong way.

We continued the chase, my feet singin' "Settin' the Pace I and II" by Dexter Gordon, Chops bragging about how "nowadays babies get up and walk soon's you drop 'em."

I told Chops to leave me alone.

Shaw 'Nuff

He finally got quiet.

"Thank you," I said, real seddity-like. I could hear Zu-Zu clapping. She always applauded performances that were strong. When confronted about anything, she would sing. And whenever Zu-Zu was without a song, she talked about "Mind Over Matter."

Humph

"It's time to see what you got," Monk said. He started stripping Zu-Zu's clothes off, trying to find her breasts.

"Good thang you ain't wearin' LA Gear," Monk said, chuckling. "I'd be here all day."

Zu-Zu shivered as Monk touched her. She sung "Black Snake Blues," then hummed "I'm Going Back to My Used to Be." She turned her head as Monk dropped saliva on her chest. She felt spittle drive down her skin, speeding up as it traveled between the two mounds. She heard the drivers discussing how flat she was. As Zu-Zu continued to get wet,

85

she opened her legs. She refused to beg Monk to stop.

"You shall reap what you sow," Zu-Zu said.

"Forget you!" Monk shouted. He pulled out a nigger flicker and stabbed her. Zu-Zu waited to exhale, then kicked the knife out of Monk's hands and watched it cut through Love.

Love was in shock. "Fuck that bitch!" he said. Then he slapped Zu-Zu across the face.

Zu-Zu Girl, confident that her man-of-war would eventually find her, spat in his face. "Love never dies," she said. No sooner than she said it, Love collapsed.

Soft Shoes

Chops pointed to the hole in my sole and the parts of my shoes that were really worn, and cracked up.

"You ain't no good," I said. "The least you could do is help a brother." I got up from the spot where I had tripped and brushed away the earth, all kinds of homeless people staring at me like I was Dr. Sinister and shit. I wanted to tell them that they had the wrong guy, that Chops was the one. I visualized him twisting the arm of the Statue of Liberty, breaking her spirit like it was nothing. I never wanted to see his face again.

My stomach was queasy. I stepped over to a street vendor and bought a cup of cool water for a dollar. I drank about one-third of the water and then poured the rest on top of my head, blue stuff trickling down through the roughest sections of my hair.

"Are you alright, mistah?" a Jewish man asked me.

"Of course," I said. "I know you didn't think that I just fell out. I was pushed. This nigger backstabber tried to dog me like I was John or Robert Kennedy."

"Sabotage," said the man, "and a damn shame, too. I always liked how Bobby stood up for you people."

For a moment, I felt like Nat Turner: I received a vision of a great five-day battle between Aryan forces and people of the Moors. I saw blood dripping from the skies, an angry red sun setting, God charging me to fight bravely, even though I would surely die. I would go out like a martyr, He promised. I would be betrayed by a Judas and left in pain under blue skies that would weep over the earth's destruction, the senseless violence, unrequited love. Like drops of rain, spit in the sky will fall in my eye, God promised. Then He disappeared, and my vision was faded.

I leaned over the short, white-skinned Jewish man and put my big, black hands on his very old wool sweater. "You seen a frail, big-mouthed black girl round here by chance? Look like a slave girl with breasts that appear to have been hit by one of Marcus Garvey's steamships. Have you seen her?" Chops stood behind me, waiting.

"You two not from the Chi-lites, are you?" the man asked. "You don't do 'Oh Girl' or nothing like that, do you? Cause my little girl likes listening to you people when you try to sing soul ballads, you know."

I wondered how a bagel, Louis Farrakhan, or a fruit of Islam would fit in his mouth. "How big is yo' mouth?" I asked him. Standing on a corner together, we made a square and looked like a black-and-white television set from the sixties. The Jewish man looked confused, like he was from the lost generation, Gertrude Stein's husband or something instead of a part of the movement of struggling people.

"You gonna answer the question or what?"

He took his eyes off me and fixed them upon a gutter. "Naw, I ain't seen no little colored girl around here," he said. "I'd remember if I'd seen something like that."

Just then Governor Cuomo drove down the street in an all-white limousine with protective glass windows, directing the wheel like he was preparing himself to do a drive-by. We really couldn't see the Governor's face, but he tossed a rainbow of confetti out of the car and hit us in the eyes with it. The Jewish dude broke out ailin'. "Up yours, asshole!" His face turned pink.

I pulled a Kleenex out of my pants pocket and tried to wipe his face. "What up with dat?" I asked. "We've been colorized, all three of us. I feel like Harold Melvin with some Blue Notes."

"I prefer The Stylistics or The Impressions or at the very least The Manhattans," the man said. Then he walked away, pigeons and hungry homeless people eating the bread crumbs that slipped out of the pocket on his sweater. An older ink-black woman pointed the white man out to a group of sooty-black Haitian and Jamaican women heaving sacks of dirty laundry and old clothes; many of them were maids or live-in nannies before they became homeless. "We bake the bread, they give us the crust," she said.

Solstice

Me and Chops had gone as far south as a man could go. I felt that I couldn't go any further. On bended knee, I lowered my big head and asked for peace.

Inner Crisis

I'm messed up.

A Shade of Jade

Inside, I am so upset that it feels like the butterflies have changed back to caterpillars, everything feeling spiny and hairy. Inside, it feels like one of those nights. If Zu-Zu could see inside my heart, she would be deeper. If Zu-Zu could feel the pain I am feeling, then she would know why.

When Can I See You Again

"Let me know," I utter. "Let me know . . . when you feel

what you feel, or if you feel like I feel."

"You don't have to worry," Chops says, standing right behind me, witnessing that single moment when the metal is ready for the maker.

Mi God Mi King

For Heaven's sake, I prayed to God for strength, courage, endurance. And I cried. Chops called me a little woman. Homeless niggas came out of the woodwork with buckets made of walnut and hard cherry oak to collect the water.

"Stolen water is sweet," said one of them.

"Just trying to save you," said another. "It is the calm and silent water that drowns a man."

"Take it and get out of here!" I shouted. I wondered what the world had come to when people didn't hesitate to snatch water. The baptism was that even an old, alcoholic brother with a shot glass came up and took a drink.

He spat most of it. "This stuff is nasty," he said. "What is it?"

"Blues," I told him.

He staggered away. "I'd rather drink the brown waste in the Harlem River," he said. "It tastes better, and it's less filling. And Nutrament makes me feel more energetic."

After he finished talking smack, he was gone. He went away looking dead like the water or the blues had killed him.

Bye Bye Blues

My mouth making O's, I waited for the oxygen to come back. Then I rose and demanded the blues to go, showing them the way out.

Blues Walk

"Why am I here?" Flukie asked Sterling Silver. They were finally headed towards the only home they knew. Flukie was ready to split Harlem. He owed everyone in the nation, including his momma. She met him and Sterling Silver at the pass to collect.

"I set that bitch up like you asked me to," she said. "I stalled her so you could get up in those trees. And I even marked her with condoms so you could take what you wanted and not have to worry about it. Now I wanna get paid. I'm here to collect." She held out her hand and waited.

Sterling Silver, who at least had a spoonful of integrity, whispered in Flukie's ear. "Pay her," he said.

"Forget you, momma," said Flukie. "You make enough already doing that gypsy shit. I ain't givin' you nothin'."

Flukie's momma pulled a gaat out of her frilly blouse and cocked it. She started out calmly. "Son," she said. "I only put you into this world because I wanted to draw welfare. I can take yo' ass right out of this world if you don't give me the motherfuckin' money you owe me!"

In a shady area of the park, Flukie pulled out of a wad of dirty money and counted off some bills. "One, two, three, four, take five," he said.

She turned and strolled away, partially stuffing the nine-millimeter back inside her bra.

Sterling Silver started moving away as well. "I'm through with this shit," he said. "If a mother would stick up her own son for five bills, there's no tellin' what she'd do to me. Yo' black-ass, blackmailing mother is headed south for the winter. When God put her in the mix, He must have envisioned her as a fruit bowl for nuts."

"Don't talk about my momma!" Flukie screamed. He picked up a rock, ran, and popped Sterling Silver on his big blackhead, on the back of his skull. Sterling Silver immediately dropped to the ground, his face pressed against the earth, his entire body soiled, blood beginning to run like a meandering river cutting straight through Harlem, a crushed Lifesaver under his right foot. Sterling Silver mumbled a few last obscenities. "Kiss my black ass, Flukie." Then he quit.

Blue Skies

"Clear sailin'," Chops said. He saw me sucking in the winds of God, and I could tell that he was up to something sneaky. Just at the moment when I was thinking "what else could possibly happen in a day among the homeless," a group of niggas pulled over to the curb in a jeep playing Black Street.

"Wanna ride?" asked the brother leaning behind the wheel. His tone and attitude brought me way back, that is, to something familiar, old school. He wore a nylon stocking over his head which I assumed was to make waves in his hair. His body was laid back.

The drugged quality of his voice could only be compared to the sluggish twang and slow drag of Hendrix, high in public but proud as hell to be spectacle. His throat projected like it had had too much acid/coke; the sound was unmistakably Cleetus', his highness. And word out on the street was that Cleetus had turned into a shermhead who had to be handled as if he were a mushroom.

Delicate matter: Chops, who I knew was Cleetus' second cousin and the black sheep of the family, appeared to recognize him immediately. He smiled right away.

"I don't think so," I said.

Chops climbed in. "Quit trippin'," he said. "These brothers can help us track down Zu-Zu. After all, how long can we keep walkin' on the good foot? My shit is blistering."

I knew that if I turned my back to walk away, Chops or Cleetus, both radicals, would probably X me right on out and make sure that I'd never come back. So quietly and reluctantly, I got in. Chops leaned into the leather back seat and started handing out Snickers, everyone copping a silent attitude and appearing on the moody side.

Blues in the Closet

Cruising past the stop sign, the apple-looking jeep rolled up on the curves of a big-ass street crowd like it wanted a piece, its booming system playing "Let The Beat Hit 'Em," a skinny brother behind the wheel sportin' a 125th Street Blood gangster lean and passin' a bomb around to his posse like he was doing a spaghetti western, niggas strapped and loading clips, black arms and legs hanging out on the side. Chops bit nervously into his nuts and whispered to me "this is a journey into sound," while I drew stick pictures of Zu-Zu with the crayon I had used earlier. As if we were being steered by a devil, we both paid extra attention to what was going on in the street.

"Just watch," said Cleetus. His boy in the front seat tossed each of us a ski mask, which Chops immediately put on.

Outside the Highbridge Garden Homes in the South Bronx, an Old Gangster (O.G.), wearing the blues and down with O.P.P., looked for an open window without bars, his nose sniffing out the dope coming his way, his big black feet feeling ice and begging him to boogie-oogie-oogie-til-he-just-can't-boogie-no-more since his crayon-colored weapon was no match for a "street sweeper." He froze on the walk, his small gun feeling increasingly more inferior.

In the mean time, a Fruit of Islam brother strolled outside of a nearby privately-owned store carrying a stack of magazines to read for escape, a Reynolds plastic-wrapped slice of bean pie easing out of his coat pocket. Looking toward the east, the Black muslim fingered through the stack and singled out an issue of the *Village Voice* which I imagined as saying that the man behind the idea of *Straight Outta Compton* is nothing more than the revolutionary Marcus Garvey in a city of angels. The brother threw the issue in the trash, his big head beginning to ache near the temple, his dark self wanting nothing more than to get out of the ghetto, a white sedan parked across the street watching his shadow fade.

Near this floundering and weak Black Muslim mumbling and cussing under his hot breath—his temple hurting, a 16-year old hip-hopper with LaTasha on her jacket was shooting crap with friends at the corner, only pausing to take the medicine she had been taking everyday of her life. Sheltered black people walked past her and straight watched LaTasha gamble with her life, her homegirls peeping the slack Muslim and making over him like he was actor Denzel Washington or they were The Honorable Elijah Muhammad's personal secretaries. One of the girls pulled out a Kool cigarette and lit up.

Like another Spike Lee joint, the hood never stopped burning, colored people always walking around on fire, hot heads seemingly everywhere, including the brother trying to maintain himself and the brother posing with the gun by a boarded-up wlndow.

A large Latin mama clutching beads and *The New Testament* (Nuevo Testamento) scurried to get out of the way, picking up on the hint that something bad was about to go down. When the jeep jumped off the curve and began charging the brother standing by the window, she screamed like a spectator not allowed to turn the corner—caught/ trapped in the middle of a bumrush. When niggas in the ride started squeezing their shit, spraying bullets like they were shots of semen, she lunged behind a red fire hydrant, blood falling on her Bible.

Like it was nothing, the jeep sped past her, people running up to the brother lying on his belly like a crab, his fingers and teeth clawing the ground.

At the back of the crowd, LaTasha suddenly had an epileptic seizure and blacked-out. One of her friends was scared to help and quickly walked away. The remaining girls scattered, hollered and screamed to get everyone's attention. As photographers, video cameras, and news cameramen curiously arrived on the scene, the latina looked at the fallen body sponging up some of the mess and tried to slowly crawl away, mumbling "Ahora vemos de manera borrosa, como en un espejo (In the same way, we can see and understand only a little about God now)...

When the assassins got several blocks away, Cleetus, the driver, pulled the jeep to the side of an alley and parked it like it was a Tonka Toy. Then, like a kid playing around with other kids in Toys R Us, he got out and headed towards the area of the shooting. Chops ripped off his ski mask and threw his gun into an open garbage bin.

"Where you think you goin'?" Chops shouted.

"I'm going to check out my work," Cleetus answered. He was walking down the street like Richard Pryor on *Which Way Is Up*, his black fire-arms flapping against both sides of his lanky body.

"Man, you stupid!" shouted a brother in the jeep. Then he repeated it, like he was DJ Kid Capri participating in a Def Comedy Jam.

Chops looked at his ski mask and wondered who thought of the idea of a criminal nigga wearing a ski mask in the first place; it was like black people assumed that only white people could ski. He threw the disguise on the floor.

"I'm getting out," he said. After the niggas called him

94

"fatboy" and "a punk," they let him go, suckas in their big mouths.

"I don't care if it costs my life," Chops yelled back. "We through, straight like that."

"God takes care of fools and babies," a nigga yelled, his hair like Don King after pulling off his stocking cap.

"Integration is an image," Chops replied, straight like that. Then he ran.

"Without us, Doughboy, you be dead in less than a year," shouted somebody.

"Look for the nigga in the mud," said somebody else. Then they put the jeep in reverse.

Before I got out of the jeep, I lifted my crayon-colored picture of Zu-Zu and flashed it so everyone could see. "Would you do this girl?" I asked.

"Get outta here before you get hurt!" they yelled, going backwards.

Still acting frightened and intimidated, Chops was sitting with me in a Bucket of Blood, a lowdown jukejoint on the bank of the Harlem River overlooking the Bronx, with a Manhattan in his hands and a pack of Kool in his hip pocket when some monkey hopped over, slapped the drink out of his hand, and snatched a bomb from the bartender and lit it, bitters all over the place and a light-skin waitress with hair like straw picking up the cherry.

Mr. Monkey showed the bomb to the crowd. At first, nobody paid him any attention.

Then, bloom! Naggas started flying everywhere like blackbirds with yellow fever trying to save their necks, one of them spitting up black vomit because he was so scared.

But, the waitress strolled up to Mr. Monkey, his heavy

right foot moody, smelly and seemingly surrounded by nits and fleas, and asked him what made him think that he had enough explosives to do her, the black-and-white television set above her big head showing a 60-second spot for *NYPD Blue*.

"Bitch," said Mr. Monkey, reaching down to scratch that foot, "I'm going to definitely fuck your ass, and when I'm through I'll set it in this cocktail glass."

He limped up to her behind, raised her little fluffy white dress, and did her. Those were hard times then: Mae West was forced into doing slapstick. Mary J. Blige was pillaged because Mr. Monkey said the jazzy vocalist owed him a favor and she replied, "I don't want to do anything." Cool Mo' D whispered "Wild, Wild West" at the end of the bar like he was surprised that Mae was offended by Mr. Monkey. Panicking, the dark cowboy beside Mo' D shouted, "It's like that, and that's the way it is." Then he ran.

Mr. Monkey finished his nasty with the "passing" waitress (that's what some other barfly wearing stirrup pants and nicknamed "Lena Horny" called her, which was like a spade calling another nigga "a spade") and then threw her out the window like it was nothing.

He smoked another nigga's fag and stabbed a ho's hand with a nigger flicker. "Anybody else want some?" he asked like this was New Jack City.

"Yea, I want some," said a negro who stood up cracking his hard knuckles like he thought he was Stokely Carmichael.

"I want some, too," said another negro who had his guitar in his hands and stood erect in the crowd like Prince in the middle of a revolution, niggas tugging at his coat of pink cashmere.

Mr. Monkey zipped up his pants, then felt for the piece

underneath his clothes. "Do you know how to use that guitar?" he asked.

"Hello." "Let's Go Crazy." "Hot Thang." "Do Me, Baby" "Gett Off." "If I Was Your Girlfriend." "I Could Never Take The Place Of Your Man." "La, La, La, He, He, Hee."

"God."

"Shockadelica."

This sick m.f. could strum an anthology of Prince's music.

"Good," muttered Mr. Monkey, reneging. "That's damn good."

The crowd whispered "punk" so Mr. Monkey could hear it.

Mr. Monkey straightened himself up. "Who wants theirs first?" he asked.

"I want it first," said the negro whose black fist shook like Mr. Lee in *Enter The Dragon*.

"Let's see what you got," said the other negro, his big guitar grinning while another nigga stuck a coin in the juke box and played "Jam On It."

Mr. Monkey reached for his stolen pocket watch, slowly set it on one of the wooden tables and popped open the electro plated lid, triggering a musical chime of "Let's Stay Together" all the niggas in the backdrop digging Al Green like they were thinking of things the way they used to be.

The ebony floor cracked underneath Mr. Monkey's heavy right boot, the mud cloth on his body slowly shaking itself free to get out of this particular fight. He flung the scary-looking African shawl over his shoulder.

"Which one of you black niggas want yo' bullet first?" he asked, motioning for Chops to stay.

"I do," said the brother, still shaking the same fist. By this time, he had stopped and picked up a can of pork-and-beans and put it in his other hand, squeezing the aluminum. Mr. Monkey reckoned he was crazy too because his mouth was white, a sure sign that he was a basehead.

"Do me first," said the other negro. His bright face was covered with rouge, and he looked ready to go from where Mr. Monkey was standing.

"Your twisted ass goes first!" said Mr. Monkey. Then he backed up a few more steps as the music ceased.

"You ever heard of 'Pop Life'?" Mr. Monkey asked, feeling for his piece again.

"Well…"

Mr. Monkey shot his ass. Next thing you know it, the negro was laid out.

"Looks like I lost a bullet," said Mr. Monkey. He leaned forward and looked down, over the man's dead body.

"Whoop, there it is," he said.

In the mean time, somebody in the house had snatched the beans, opened the can, and was scraping pork out. That finally reminded the bartender to call the coppers and beg for help. Chops remained on the stool while this monkey kept bringing the noise.

"Who else wants some?" he asked.

"Fuck you, Chiggerfoot," said the other negro. "You ain't all that."

Mr. Monkey took a deep breath and waited to exhale. A fly fell out of the air and gazed at him from the hard wood.

"You got any Tic-Tacs or peppermint patties or anything?" it asked. Flies were like that in the ghetto, or where people were homeless and desperate for food.

Mr. Monkey crushed the fly between the wood boards and his Hush Puppy boot. Then he picked up the remains with his brown roughed-up middle finger and ate it like sushi wrapped around a rice cake.

"For one piece of booty and a warm drink, I got two niggas to dis, but I'm telling you that that dirt-road white-looking woman ain't worth all of ya'll dying," said Mr. Monkey. By any means necessary, he was trying to avoid fighting this nigga.

"That trash piled on the step outside was my wife," the negro said.

Mr. Monkey glanced at Chops and me as if to say, "How was I supposed to know." He motioned for Chops to stay.

"Don't blame me," he told the negro, checking out the fury of this man. "You the one who kilt it, Lover."

"Kill him, Jim," the rest of the negroes shouted like Kelly's heroes. They were perpetrating—or, at the very least, perpetuating.

"I'm straight outta Brooklyn, Boss," said the negro. "I beat the stew out of niggas who mess with my wife."

Mr. Monkey pointed to the drinking hole's broken window and shattered glass, the whore on the bank of the river all laid out on her dead ass.

"Look here, Jim or John Brown, or whatever your name is, why get bent out of shape over this heap of passing ship? You'd have to catch the vapors to make her boiler work."

"It's a black thang, you must understand," said the negro. "To you, I am a black kung fu star. But to her, I was her main man." It took another nigga to call him out and restore his sense of rhythm.

"Jim, Jim," said Mr. Monkey. "Do you know who I am? I'm your Marsa King, your daddy-o, your big, fat momma, and your spoonful of Spam." Mr. Monkey felt like he was in a *Game Of Death*.

"Man, you come straight out of a comic book," Jim replied.

"Word," Mr. Monkey said. "But I like that picture of Queen Latifah on the wall and that catchy slogan underneath her, 'Rock Dis Funky Joint.'"

"I hope you believe in God," added Mr. Monkey, "cause I've already said 'goodnight' to sweet Prince and now it's yo' turn to fight the devil."

"Hell ain't nothing but brimstone that blackens a nigger's feet," said Jim. "You got to come with more than that to put me asleep."

Mr. Monkey once again pointed to the trash outside seemingly just drifting alongside the contaminated bank. "I blew out her candle and threw her out the door. But now I've got more ashes to pile on top of that horror/whore."

"Let's get down!" said Jim. Everybody got up and started dancing like the time was Disco and Heatwave had said "Boogie Nights" twice.

Me and Chops were about to get up when Mr. Monkey peeped us again and motioned for us to stay. So we sat, tight, and watched a 1 a.m. re-broadcast of the late news on television, whitey promising fair conditions starting Sunday. The broadcast flipped to a wide shot of busy Wall Street while the weatherman discussed details.

Mr. Monkey gestured for the nigga by the jukebox to drop in another coin. Greedily, the jukebox swallowed the coin—it didn't matter if the money was dirty—and belched out Bessie Smith's "It's Dirty But It's Good," the scratchy blues beginning to get under everybody's skin.

Looking irritated, Jim stepped closer to Mr. Monkey. Mr. Monkey tossed him a piece of Juicy Fruit chewing gum.

"I'm about two seconds off your black ass," Mr. Monkey said.

"Whatever," said Jim.

"When the music quits, I'm going to blow a hole in your head big enough to carry your dick around."

"Whatever."

"When the music quits, I'm going to wax you and then use you as my calling card."

Jim sprinted to the jukebox and kicked in its belly. While his back was turned, Mr. Monkey filled him with hot bullets; they was cussing and tearing up his skin like a lover's fingernails. Jim let out a scream, then closed his eyes for good, eighty-sixed.

"You shot him in the back!" one of the negroes shouted from under a table.

"So I did," Mr. Monkey yelled back. "Just another day in the hood. Who cares? What of it?"

"You did a nice job," said one of the negroes.

"Yea, Jungle Jim there looks real good," said another negro. "His blood oozes out of those holes like brown honey in a Queen B."

"Yes, you did a sweet job," agreed a third negro.

"Shut up then," said Mr. Monkey. He stepped over to the bartender and asked for a sour.

"Drink in good health, asshole," said the bartender. He passed Mr. Monkey the drink in a broken glass.

Mr. Monkey stared at Chops, who was eating his fingernails and waiting for the T.V. news to mention the drive-by and the bloody murder of a black man earlier that day, white shirts and satin dresses stampeding out of the bar while they still had a chance.

"Check yo' self," said Mr. Monkey, all up in Chops' face, his breath spoiled by alcohol.

"I just want to be," said Chops. He got up and nervously strolled away, visibly further disturbed by the fact that his cameo never showed up on television.

"Punk-ass bitch," said Mr. Monkey.

I raised up and showed Mr. Monkey my picture, wrinkles in Zu-Zu's face like she was starting to get very tired. "Do you know where I could check to find this bitch?"

Mr. Monkey chased me back out into the street.

After being harrassed by "New York, New York" while passing hummy fades strung out on the crowded street, me and Chops hitched another ride — this time to the East River with a poorly-educated young white woman, probably no older than twenty-one, who said she was looking for a big man. In her Ford pick-up truck, she sucked on cigarettes, staring at every black butt and smiling at Chops sitting next to her. She drank a can of Nutrament for an aphrodisiac.

"Like one?" she finally asked.

"No," said Chops. She looked surprised, then played it real cool, singing "Freak Me." Chops pulled out a plastic container of old Excedrin PM and took four, losing the safety cap in the seat, all the white powder inside his body beginning to make him trip.

She popped in a tape of Kenny G singing something about "nightime at Tribeca." Then, as if the song wasn't appropriate, she ejected the cassette and pushed in another Kenny G tape and blasted "One Night Stand."

"Is there anything you want?" she asked. She was talking out the side of her neck and the sound was loud but not clear.

"Yea," Chops answered. "Take me to see Liberty Enlightening The World."

"Think we got 'nuff gas to get to da harbor?" she asked. She talked worse than a nigga from The Valley. Chops shook his big head.

"Why don't we just drive straight to Sugarhill?" she asked. "It's all good."

"Somebody asked you to be creative?" Chops asked. He wanted her to stay out of his mix.

"Ofay," she seemed to say. "You don't have to get so jumpy about it. What's the problem? Don't you like me?" She rewound the tape and the cigarette between her lips stopped dancing.

"Say 'hi' to the bad guy," said Chops. He pointed at his self.

She could see right through him. "The soul that knows itself is opaque," she said, putting her right hand on his crotch. But she later rambled and admitted that a nigga had showed her the quotation in Bruce Lee's chapter "It's Just A Name."

When they got to the harbor, Chops told her to pull over. I quickly pushed open the door and jumped off the seat. Chops was going to kiss her goodbye but got more than he expected when she stuck him with the tip of a Papermate pen while his back was turned and he was getting out of the truck.

As soon as he got off the truck, Chops turned around and looked in disbelief. "Backstabber!" He thought of the O'Jays saying that word over and over again in their song.

"You should of did me when I gave you the chance," she said. "Cleetus told me to send you a forget-me-not, to help you to remember. But I would of let you alone if you had just talked to me; sweetness is my weakness."

This ain't *Boomerang*!" said Chops, taking control of the pen. "I don't see anything funny. You tried to lay me down to sleep."

She pointed to Chops' beltline. "Quit bitchin'. It would take more than that to do that tub of lard."

Before she could leave, I raced back over to the window

and waved the picture of Zu-Zu in her face. "Did you have a one-night stand with this thin black girl, by chance?"

"Mister, do I look like I'm into drag?" She threw the truck into overdrive and, with a cigarette still going strong in her mouth, burned some rubber, Chops trying to get his stuff together while another white woman watched us from nearby.

In the hood, if somebody sends you a message, he's going to back it up. It was with good reason that Chops, clearly struggling to be a boy in the hood, was visibly shaken. He sat on the dock of the bay squeezing his peace/piece. After eyeing the colossal copper woman crowned in front of our faces, he looked at the white woman creeping backwards and said, "You ain't gotta go, but you got to get the hell outta here." She flew.

As soon as she was gone, Chops cracked up.

Like God commands everyone to do, I went into the closet and prayed. I asked God to forgive Chops, who was swearing that I would regret ever knowing him. He shouted profanity until I was no longer in sight, making sure I heard him loud and clear. "You left me alone," he screamed at the end.

I Hear A Rhapsody

Someone on the street is singing "City Girl" by Ronnie Laws. From what I remember of Zu-Zu's diary, I believe it's her song. I move the crowd, a few people disturbed by my pushing and shoving calling me names like "Rude Boy" and "Sound Chaser."

O Amor En Paz

"Zapp!" I shouted. I wanted all the bad and ugly things in my life to go away. I wanted to be an African distance runner in a second life. I was skinny, but I couldn't run very fast or long. I needed more bounce to the ounce.

"Zapp!" I shouted. I tried to work hoodoo and juju like they were Play Dough in my hands.

Palm Grease

Zu-Zu watched two fingers rub and tug on her black nipples before she finally spoke again. "Mistah, if you don't take yo' greasy fingers off my breasts, I'm gonna smoke you," she said. She used her feet to drag Love along the line of grass and hard liquor, occasionally stopping to kick him upside his head and crotch as he scooted along the ground trying to feel her.

"The thrill is gone, baby," said Zu-Zu. Then she spat towards his face.

Monk, being the low-down snake he was, recoiled and stared at himself in one of those rare moments where he freaked out and checked his own program to see if maybe he, too, had a rubber stamp on his tail. "Sometimes you can't let go," he said, "of the love you thought was yours, mine and yours."

Zu-Zu only listened because she sort of liked the fact that what Monk was saying seemed to come from a ballad. In deep thought, she saw herself crazy in love with only Monk trying to stop her. She slapped him on the face.

"What you do that for?" Monk asked. His face was a tart cherry. He started to whine and cry but shut up and grabbed his crotch when he realized that his posse was still looking on. All of the black cowboys were grabbing their crotches, too.

"This grabbing our crotches must be a black thang," said Monk. He did a cock-of-the-walk stride as if a King Cobra was between his legs. He buzzed and hummed around Zu-Zu like her name was "Sweet Sue" and the song was "Me So Horny."

"I can give you anything, Honey, but you got to give to

receive," he said.

Zu-Zu kicked Love again. "The world passing by my window don't mean nothing to me," she said. "Touch me again and I'll smoke you."

Monk pulled a stolen rice bowl out of his pants and tossed it like a doily into the hands of a tall tree. "Shaka Zulu!" he said. "Chaka Khan! Shabba Ranks! In other words, let no man pull you so low as to make you hate him."

Zu-Zu laughed. "I can't believe you'd say some stale stuff like that," she said. "You can find more convincing lines at the unemployment office. You ain't ever gonna get you some unless you learn how to rap better than that."

"Skip it then," said Monk. "Let's just get on with it."

Love was embarrassed. He looked Monk straight in the eye and shot himself in the foot, tired of being kicked in the face by Zu-Zu.

"It's a time for martyrs," said Monk. He snatched Zu-Zu by her smelly hair and right nipple and lifted her up for his boys to witness his power.

"It's easy to pick her up by a nipple," said Dart, "but can you do two?"

Monk put Zu-Zu down and sized up her chest, his jawbone clicking but not a single dentist around willing to take care of the problem before getting paid.

"To do that, I'd have to be able to fint it," he said. As expected, the wisecrack got a jolt out of his boys who were such simple creatures, their teeth also clicking.

During the hearty ribbing, Dart slid a note to another cowpoke that read "I'm getting sic and turd of laffing at all his stupitt jokes."

"Boys," said Monk, "Freak-a-zoids, let's do her!"

Zu-Zu screamed. "Stop!" she said. "I ain't afraid of you

motherfuckers! But before you do me, just tell me which one of you is going first so I can send that man home to his momma with a special gift from me."

Zu-Zu started scratching her body. You could see the fear in the eyes of Monk's boys. They started backing off.

"Hold up!" Monk shouted. "She's bluffing!"

"I'm unfaithful," said Zu-Zu. "My favorite role is being Butch and the Sundance Kid."

"She's a bi!" Dart shouted. "I can't play dat!" He tore away.

Monk ripped out his penis and proceeded to do her until Zu-Zu lifted her chin.

"Stop!" Zu-Zu shouted again. "I ain't afraid of you! But if you brave enough to risk your life trying to do me, be brave enough to at least wear a condom, one that is dated and lubricated with spermicide."

"How much do they cost?" Monk asked.

"You can go down to Planned Parenthood and get a bagful free."

"Not enough time," said Monk. "I'm starting to get soft."

"Sooner or later, it had to happen," said Zu-Zu. "No man can stay hard forever."

Monk zipped up his pants and fell down to the ground. "What am I going to do now?" he asked. Then he closed his eyes and laid out. Zu-Zu chuckled, then spat on his tan as the sun began to set. She sung "Show Me The Way To Go Home."

Tinkle, Tinkle

After stopping to urinate in the weeds and pieces of broken glass in a small field behind a liquor store, I continued my search for Zu-Zu. As I ran, I discovered another hole in my sole. I noticed my self bleeding.

For Heaven's Sake

I kept going.

Propulsion

Still carrying the rock that he popped Sterling Silver on the head with, the stone that was now stained with Silver-blood and resting in a sweaty hand, Flukie caught a subway train, sat down on the cushion seat and began to conjure up ways he could take out his momma. He cracked up when James Brown's "Payback" came on the Brooklyn radio station.

Killer Joe

That's what Flukie was. He looked over to a brown dude propped up and relaxed next to him, temporarily enjoying the ride.

"Ah'mah kill her, Joe," Flukie said.

"That's yo' business," the man said, grinning at a young white woman who was rolling apples at his feet. "Leave me out of it."

As the car traveled through the tunnel screaming, Flukie went past the poor children of the ghetto like they were nothing. He rode the train on out, thinking about both his momma and rocks.

Birthdays and Funerals

For me, sticking together was what finding Zu-Zu was really about. If I didn't try to save her, she would surely become just another statistic. Her death at the hands of those gangbangers would be just another day in the hood.

Under a Blanket of Blue

The police shook their big heads and zipped up the black bag containing Sterling Silver's body, and the paramedics took him away like a breath of fresh air. Niggas at the scene rolled themselves in the chalk and put on a black minstrel show to try to forget the whole thing. They played old music to protest the violence, including "Ballad for Very Tired and Very Sad Lotus Eaters."

Echoes of Harlem

People without melanin were frightened throughout the five burroughs.

Five Pennies

"You got to be kidding!" shouted Chops, holding up a smalltime grocery store. "I know you've got to have more than that! Give all the money you have, or I'll do your wife and three little suckers for free!" Chops stuck the tip of a steak knife in the white woman's throat.

"Poke her, and you're not going to make it out of the ghetto alive, nigger!" said the husband. Then he upped his dough, contemplating if he should reach for the silent alarm behind the counter.

"Watch me," said Chops, counting the bills and feeling more and more like a liberated black man.

Using Nutrament to ward off AIDS, he did the wife anyway because she had breasts like Zu-Zu's. Then he flew.

Scuttlebutt

"You'll pay for this!" promised Whitey. But by this time, Chops had the juice.

The Morning After

There was blues in the news. On Crime Stoppers, police announced a $1,000 reward for information leading up to the capture of the man who got Sterling Silver. Several niggas at Sam's Furniture Store in Harlem took off their sterling silver ropes and chains, and then called the coppers to talk.

Bouncing With Bud

One woman came over from the stoop and offered to do me, her hair wet with malt liquor. She swore that it would help me feel better. I paused by a red light and searched for a condom, Zu-Zu still on my mind. The trick refused to wait. She gave me her card, a piece of cardboard with her number, and split.

My Funny Valentine

Back in February when Zu-Zu and I first met, she gave me a bagful of imperial hearts. I remember my mouth gaping, Zu-Zu handing hearts to me even though I didn't deserve them.

Since Zu-Zu was always asking for time, I gave her a lost-and-found wristwatch with a pink plastic band.

For real: Zu-Zu said that the exchanging of gifts was all about black unity. But, I believe it was also an action that she concocted in order to one day check and see if I still had a heart and could accept life as a process where certain measures are taken to build spirituality.

Steps

Trying to rub it in, a young black man with hair like wool struts past me singing "all I see is your love." One of Sam's windows shatters, glass falling on people's babies and children on a crushed velvet sofa outside the store.

Hollering and screaming and carrying-on, Sam goes to find his momma. Wearing "Christopher" on the front of his shirt and "The Real Deal" on the back, the very bright-skinned man stops singing and stares right back at me.

"What's yo problem, nigga?"

"I'm trying to hold on to my heart," I reply.

"What is this, love story? Raise yo' black behind up and keep movin'."

When Christopher spots Sam approaching the front door with a big momma, he starts running. "I'm on the go, G! I can't look back!"

I kiss Sam's big-ass momma goodbye and then sprint away as well, thinking of how Chris-man face's is so bright that his whole presence hits you like a visit from a policeman's or

110

a rent-a-nigga's flashlight.

Let's Get Right

Perhaps a day late and a dollar short, I'm talkin' in tongue, Zu-Zu darting through my mind while I race past another blurry crowd of street people crapped out, kicked to the curb, and straight up paying their dues. A few spooks doing a ghost dance attempt to reach out and touch my clothes for some sort of good luck ritual like going ovah. "The spirits are in control of you now," one of them says. It's like all of my heart and all of my running and chasing is for trickeration.

I hear other abusive men on the stoops overseeing Central Park branging the noise and shouting to their wives that "the chickens have come home to roost." As I slow down, they stick their hands in their pockets and front having a gauge to discourage me from running in their direction. About eight young black teenage girls, probably freaks who gave up sex to get into a gang, scream "go-man-go." Hawking, I notice that most of them appear to be single mommas clinging to welfare checks and Twinkies like it's Mother's Day, a few picking at the marks on their bodies where gang initiation seems to have scarred them for good.

Let's Get Right

I am hit by Kinesia. (For about a week and before I became homeless, I tried to get into medical school.) I begin to run at a slower pace 'cause my heart is going up and down like it's hanging on a string. I am exhausted, frustrated, and mad. I can't kill nothin' and won't nothin' die. Inside my mind, I keep hearing that trash talk from my days playing alley ball—niggas with hops checking me on the concrete court, repeatedly asking if I got the love while the dump trucks collected the garbage.

It Was Inside That I Cried

I thought of Zu-Zu who never seemed to show love for anything, but always contended that she felt it.

Sometimes I Cry

I usta tell Zu-Zu, but it's not like I'm a Will Downing or anything. Zu-Zu would glare at me like yeah-right. Being extremely sensitive to everything, I would sluggishly move away as if I had Down's Syndrome.

Stop, In The Name of Love

Zu-Zu saw me jogging alongside the edges of the park. "Where you going?" she asked. I had almost gotten past her. She stretched out, extending her body to get in my way. I bent over and quickly untied her.

"You go, boy!" she shouted, skinnin and grinnin.

Pretending to be called by God, Monk woke up and grabbed his gaat by the shade tree, hoppergrass on his face and the memory of using Buddha grass and submission still fresh in his mind. He started firing ballistics.

"You did that on purpose!" I shouted to Zu-Zu. I tried to think of how I could sweet talk my way out of this one.

"Yep, she gave you the oke-doke," said Monk, stylin' and profilin', ready to throw a brick. "Leap, if you feel froggy."

Zu-Zu laughed like she didn't mean to bust my game. That's what I liked about Zu-Zu; she was always looking out for number one. Once, she hooked up with a Sugar Daddy and got into an after hours affair where she told some old head to off me for "harraigning" her.

"I would never harraign you," I told Zu-Zu pretending to be down-for-mine. "God don't like ugly." Then I slipped away and looked the word up in the dictionary. The closest word I could find was "harrying," which meant to harass, worry, or torment.

Well, then I realized that maybe Zu-Zu was right. I'd

torment her until she sings "My Man" like Billie Holiday-woman.

"That's asking an awful lot from a little colored girl," Zu-Zu usta say in one of those rare moments where she would downplay her own skills. "Lady sings the blues."

"But she can't showboat like you, Zu-Zu. Your breasts are mahogany, and your dream book has always been 'do you know where you're going to, do you like the things that life's been showing you?'"

"I only know why caged birds sing," Zu-Zu said. She read me a Paul Laurence Dunbar poem called "Sympathy."

"You got this race woman stuff down pat," I said.

"You know what time it is," said Zu-Zu. She crinkled the paper like it was hair in a hot-comb and stuck the half-done ball in my mouth.

"You scank."

"Say what? Oh, no you didn't call me a skeezer." Zu-Zu spat in my face.

"Looks like your savior done jumped salty on you," Monk said to Zu-Zu, hyping it up. Then his jaws got tight. "I'm through wit you, painted woman. Take a chill pill. Take low and go before I wax some ass."

Zu-Zu scatted. She took Love with her.

"America's problem is us!" I shouted to her.

Monk grabbed my naps and started going upside my big head, straightening out the kinks. Spinning around like a scratched up LP, I saw Zu-Zu moving quick, fast, and in a hurry.

Monk stood with his gun sellin' woof tickets and his right fist clenched and shaking, trying to work my nerves. "Scram!" he yelled.

I refused to budge.

Monk reached into his dashiki and slipped out a ginsu

113

knife. "Don't make me none…be prepared to die then." He visualized himself as the Bruce Lee story, the crow, the last dragon.

Homefolks, with cockroaches and all, came dashing out of their houses and apartments in the hood, the rest looking out to Central Park from their cribs and through the bars, looking down to the street from balconies and ledgers, looking between men's trousers and women's lingerie, some of them blowing like they were partying while holding cocktails and giving the choke sign. Even Chris-man came back, like he had been resurrected or born again.

Monk took a bow and then got down to business. He swung his knife, but missed. In front of a group of hollering women and rough-necks, I snatched his wrist and smuggled the black blade inside his chest. Blood fell out.

Chris-man stepped up to him and started yelling in his face. "Those who live by the sword, shall die by the sword!"

I bear witness that you are a bad nigga," said one of the hoochie mommas. "You are all that, and then some."

"Yep," I said. "All yaw can go home now. It's over." After poking their fingers in the blood to see if it was real or catsup, they slowly drifted away, chattering, like spectators in the old Roman coliseum, niggas playin' follow-the-leader—sayin' "when in Rome, do as the Romans do." I heard young niggas with guns tucked securely inside their pants laughing and saying stuff like "welcome to the terror dome." Believing they were Public Enemy raising Cain, they refused to leave. Instead, they searched for a place to sit down and get full off shots and forties, oil and tude finally coming out of the bag.

"They'll never rise beyond this," said Chris-man, dusted.

"Wherever a black man goes, that's Harlem," I said.

For some reason, Chris-man launched into a speech: "Our

sistas have given their lives for these fools, twenty-foe-seven. But the white man has got us under a mojo. Everythang is everythang, but we've got to quit this he-say-she-say, and slippin and slidin. We up south. The watermelon we cut up carries the black seeds of slaves. Lawd, have mercy."

"Chris-man, cut somebody some slack. You act like you caught the vapors. Since this ain't our turf, take a chill-pill ."

Chris-man gave me the soul shake and shook the cobwebs out of his head; they clung to me like white on rice. "These young brothas just don't know what they doin'," he said.

After that, Chris-man motored away and disappeared, and I never saw his bright self again. But his momma came out of the crib to look for him. They say she even checked the gypsy tent in the park without wearing a plastic bag over her jheri curl so the chemicals would stink up the place or the crystals would get caught in her hair as proof for the police.

With Monk put in check, I searched again for Zu-Zu. Girl had moved the crowd, like that.

"You ain't nothin' but a ho, bitch!" I shouted before remembering what she always said, "You reap what you sow, go for what you know." I stopped to think twice about calling her those names.

Then I went on. "Fuhgit," I said. "Forget her."

When I spun around to walk back to the gypsy tent myself, I caught Chops glaring between the bars of some old house like a dog. He had listened to everything. He began counting dead presidents and doing freaky statues-of-liberty with his fingers.

Straight Ahead

Blue light specials popped up seemingly out of nowhere. I started half-steppin', white cops sneering and watching our every move, Chops feeling for his nine while laying dead, them dirty blues all around us.

Brief Hesitation

The police weren't sure if they wanted to take a nigga in front of so many other black people. They were scared. They decided to lay back and ask me some questions first.

"Anybody seen who killed the ugly black nigger a few yards away?" they asked. "Since we are already on what you people call Colored Peoples' Time, we are going to give you a few moments to think about it before we start busting all of you people for causing an obscene disturbance in a public sector. How does jail without bond sound to you savages? We can have you speaking pidgin languages all over again. We have the authority to incarcerate a rainbow, including Jesse Jackson's National Rainbow Coalition." Two of the police were standing with a hand on the hip and the other on a billy club, their red necks twisting around to avoid the black super flies and make sure that nobody would steal on them.

Indestructible

Front and center, I strolled off, too black, too strong, to stop and give the coppers an answer.

Bye Bye Blues

I left them boys hot and bothered.

Good Bait

Acting like I was a scholar, I knew that I could count on seeing them boys again.

I Could Write A Book

Like that, I could blow the whistle on those filthy pigs. While brothas and sistas rallied and gathered around me in the street, I picked up my hip with a cat walk.

"Just Squeeze Me,

And I'll trick."

When or Where

It didn't matter.

Without A Song

I refused to go out like a sucker. I did.

Black Narcissus

I wanted to break somebody's face. If truth be told, I didn't think I could care about somebody any longer. I didn't even care whether I lived or died. I felt like I had gotten a nose job and nutted out. All I wanted was a song.

Adios

I waved to the crowd and looked all around for my crimey. I could feel Chops stirring up trouble somewhere, tracking me from a distance.

Stormy Weather

I could see the dark cloud hanging over my big head.

"I'm Gonna Go Fishin'"

I mumbled to myself. Niggas heard rumbling throughout Harlem and then some. It sounded like the liberty bell had broke and The City of Brotherly Love couldn't get it togetha. A few niggas running claimed it sounded like God dancing on a natural high: With every snap of His fingers, lightning strikes the tallest trees and sweat pours from His face, they said. Harlemites scurried to get away from hell/hail, women scampering with skillets over their hair, black men tripping.

Chops, as sneaky as he was, followed me, hiding wherever he could. I saw his fat face peek around the tit of an Afrikan woman on a stoop, her hungry baby girl crying as if startled by Chops' treachery, dread in control.

For a minute, I broke my stride, bent down, and picked up a paper before it got destroyed by the weather. Then I read:

The Wall Street Journal, "What's News," 75 cents, circulation 1,935,713…"**The White House declared** that 'its patience is wearing thin' on Haiti and that Haitian leaders can avoid a U.S.-led invasion only by stepping down'…'BLOOD, NOT 'BRIDGES,' lures Japanese tourists."

I crushed the paper and shot the wad towards Chops, who seemed surprised to know that I could see him.

"You gone?" he asked, trying to play it off.

"What you think, man?" Chops was basically an educated fool, and I was finally starting to lose my patience with him.

"Where you goin', nigga?"

I just wanted Chops to get off my case. He was still hypin' that same old nigga-shit, proof that you can't teach an old dog new tricks. "Look for me in the whirlwind of the storm," I told Chops.

Chops beat his own face. "Let the drummer get wicked," he said. "Before you go, make sure I get to say goodbye."

Sunset
Strange Vibes
Every Evening
Madness/Wicked Blues

"You gonna need my help," I told Chops. "I should care, but I don't. It bees dat way sometimes." I turned my back to Chops and started walking away.

Big Dog

Chops screamed. Then he called me out and swore. "I'll be back," he said. He drank a can of Nutrament to stave off the muscle spasms in his back and stomach.

A few niggas inside their cribs must have thought Chops' shouted "baby got back" 'cause they started looking out of their windows. Men playing spades told their wives that Chops shouted "get back." Pimps strutted out into the street like Chops had called them "sharp as a tack." Women flaunting their coochies spread the word and gossiped that Chops said that, as long as they didn't cut off his dick and throw it out in the yard, they were "welcomed to attack." Little children said that Chops shouted "don't give me no flack." Young geez got mad 'cause they thought Chops accused them of trying to mack. Dope pushers living in the street ran over to sell Chops their part of the crack. The Chops' fan club went around and set the record straight. Members hyped that Chops got riled and frankly told me what I could do with Zu-Zu. They claimed Chops wound up saying "fuck that." Word got back to me that Chops, backed by Cleetus, warned niggas in the barrio to know their station in life and never leave it. "Every dog has its day," niggas advised me, "leave him to his."

All Night Blues (Death Rain)

Everywhere I roamed, I had to keep on keepin' on, and to keep checking my back. I waited for niggas to jump me. I prayed to find Zu-Zu before something happened. All night, I mumbled verses from the Song of Solomon, wishing that Zu-Zu would be my woman, the sky smoking and full of thunder as if God was burning up about creating earth and stomping His feet in His own house. Although many of the homeless were still hanging out in the park, niggas' motions were downbeat. Everybody was singing the blues, trying to curl up to a good fire. Several times during the night, God released his rage and fury, repeatedly spitting on stray pieces and strawberries in the park. Even niggas used to floodin' prayed for a better day.

Early Morning Blues

The closest beauty shop where women could gather to rap, network, talk shit, and provide support for one another was Toni's, which happened to be next door to a black-owned barber shop. I decided to check out the scene in case Zu-Zu turned up. I walked into Toni's first, asking for Zu-Zu Girl. I never saw so many black women bust out laughin' so hard. "Who dat?" one younger woman asked. "Sounds like one of them Shaka Zulu lookin' warrior-bitches."

Another woman stuck her head out of the hair dryer and pointed at the sign listing the prices for ladies' facials and French manicures. "Honey, I think you in the wrong place. You need to take the beauty supplies to the back."

I quickly escaped. Then I went into the men's barber shop. The barbers paid me no attention. They kept right on clipping and combing hair like it was nothing. Brothers were talking with toothpicks in their mouths and chit-chatting like women while waiting to sit in the barber's chair, one dude asking, "who moved the toilet?"

"Why you care?"

"You damn right, I got me some. Long as she's not my sister, I don't care."

"What you say? Did you say you don't care. Alright, you gone mess around and get that jungle fever."

"Ain't nothin' worse than a white girl. They'll trail you wherever you go."

"Say, you might wanna wash out that Dudley's next time, befo' you come in here. You'll get a cleaner cut, my man."

"Who next? Nigga, grab some cushion."

"Where the Preacher at?"

"Seem like his black ass be gone 365 days a year."

"Nigga don't ever come to work. Ask him when he gonna clip some hair. Shit, I saw him yesterday mackin' to a couple of tenderonies."

"If you see the nigga again, tell him he betta' be forgettin' about those strawberries in the street and gettin' his ass to the shop. Hell, we got all these big heads in here, everybody coming inside and lookin' for parts."

"Hey, hey. Did anyone get the chance to see on T.V. that brother who iced Michael Jordan's father? He dead, man. They gonna kill him in prison. He ain't goin' nowhere."

"Last thing you wanna do is molest somebody's children or hurt someone from the outside that inmates respect."

"Since when did yaw start charging $8.50 for a fade?"

"We had no choice. Got to pay the bills. It costs us bank just to park across the street. Meter man won't give us a break."

"Yeah, but seem like everytime I come in here, it be crowded."

"Shut up, nigga. You only come in here once a month."

"Can't afford to come more. When yaw going to get a pop machine."

"Soon as you come in here twice a month for a fade. Now shut up, nigga."

One of the barbers stopped clipping momentarily and swept the floor. "You niggas got some nappy shit."

"You next, young man. What can I do for you?"

He grabbed a pair of rusty scissors and a bottle of after-shave, talking to no one in particular. "Did you know Harlem used to be controlled by the Irish before crimey niggas took over? I remember the day when the cops wouldn't even ride through this neighborhood. Now they eat lunch at the corner."

Zu-Zu must have seen my big head waving in the shop. She opened the door as wide as possible, ringing the cow bell (most brothers were cool enough to just slip in through a crack), and snatched me to go outside.

"What are you doing here?" Zu-Zu asked.

"What do you mean what am I doing here? What you

121

doing here? I thought you was so content to run away for good. And by the way, don't ever spit in my face again. You dig me?"

"I couldn't. Word on street is that Chops went off for a few dollars more, and that you taking no shorts, and that you a dead man, even though you tried to squash it."

"Yeah, clearly Chops is flakey now," I said.

"He's always been flaky," said Zu-Zu. "It's just that you couldn't see it. From jump, Chops sold you out. In exchange for a knot, Chops agreed to let Cleetus ride down on you, although Cleetus would have surely performed the one-eight-seven on Chops if he had tried to resist."

"Why couldn't he just flee or stay low like a smooth criminal?"

"Can't. Too paranoid. Plus some dick-whupped white white hoochie momma put a baby on the man, made him think that he needed the money to sponsor her."

"Whassup with that?" I asked.

"She working a spot for Cleetus now," Zu-Zu answered. "Says she needs the funds to buy cigarettes."

"Where did you get all of this smack from?"

"The ladies talking in the beauty shop," Zu-Zu said. "I went in there to see how much it would cost to get a new relaxer. You just got to listen to women; they know things."

"Where can a homeless nigga go? What's going to happen between us, Zu-Zu?" I pulled out my shrinking crayon and crossed out somebody's shit on the sidewalk, drawing a heart around it.

"What the hell he doin'?" one barber asked the other. He was looking at us through the window, giving us the red eye.

"I can't tell for sure, but I think the brother was writing something on your sidewalk."

"I don't want none of that gangbangin' mess around here. The boys would bust up my place."

"Maybe he's singing his life's story?"

The senior barber shook his matted gray hair. "Naw. That'd be about as stupid as writing a novel about a barber shop in Harlem. Tell 'em to get away from my shop."

The taller barber dropped his scissors, wiped his hands on a white towel, opened the door, and stepped outside. "Ho, you ain't got to go," he said. "But you got to get the hell out of here."

Zu-Zu moved closer to him, then, on her tiptoes, spat in his face, his long, thick moustache harboring lakes of spittle, destroying his dream of appearing in an Afro Sheen commerical. I grabbed Zu-Zu, and we ran away before he could hurt her, my girl all out of whack and singing "Hot Child in the City."

"You got him good and that ain't bad," I told Zu-Zu. I sounded like her.

"Nobody calls me a ho, like I got love for sale." Zu-Zu sounded like me.

Farewell Blues

Zu-Zu wanted to be a romantic. She squeezed my hand and led me in the direction of the gypsy tent. She said it was time to quit running the streets.

"How are we supposed to do that?" I asked. Zu-Zu said that she would tell me tomorrow.

"Tomorrow may be too late," I said. I got this Winans' song in my head. They're the same group who sung "Bring Back The Days of Yea and Nea."

We jogged to a bench near the blue tent and sat down in front of a wooden crate that people had used to eat cheese on. We could still smell the nasty scent.

123

"You know what?" Zu-Zu asked. She went off in the conversation as if she was doing a ballad. "If I could just take a little time out, can I do that? 'Cause I wanna lay my cards right on the table. You see, sometimes, when it's late at night, after the show, I sit here, and I dream and I dream and I dream. And although I know that I usta dream the impossible, you see, your love was impossible."

"But you never stopped dreaming, Zu-Zu."

"Oh no, oh no."

"You never stopped dreamin'."

"Like Bessie Smith, this Girl takes the best of what life has to offer."

"Play it easy."

"Singing in the faces of men, I can take a single hit and use it to stuff the same old tired bra that I wear."

"Keet it right there."

"I go around pretendin' to wear a B cup."

"When are you gonna say it's alright, baby girl?"

"I don't want us to live any longer like this," Zu-Zu whispered. She lifted my yellow hand and placed it over her left breast which had long collapsed under pressure. She was ready to go.

"My funny valentine," I said just before she swep me away, her heart skipping and beating irregularly.

Longing for Home

"I'm goin' home," Zu-Zu said.

"A house in not a home," I told Zu-Zu. It was for simply supermarket conversation. The slow jam we had just sang on the bench made me feel like a star, like Luther Vandross.

Squeezing my hand and leading me all the way, Zu-Zu charged the tent like she wanted to see if the gypsy woman could read our future. She screamed when we got close to the entrance of the tent, S.O.S. coming out of her mouth. Someone had shot the gypsy woman, shoved the crystal ball between her thick lips, and thrown her outside of the tent.

"O' God!" Zu-Zu screamed. Flukie came running out of the tent, knocking her to the ground. Flukie flew, shouting, "You next, homeboy, you next!"

For The Cool In You

Zu-Zu picked up my hand and again placed it over her heart. "This is for the cool in you," she said. "Don't listen to that nigga. Let's just go. Let's not do anything foolish now. Those niggas are just trying to survive. We're all the same."

I was about to say that this was an A and B conversation and that, if she really wanted to talk about other niggas trying to survive, she could see her way out of it. But a stable of little black boys and little black girls suddenly raced over and asked us what happened. "Is she dead?" they asked, holding their noses.

"Long gone," I replied.

"What you do comes back to you," Zu-Zu warned them. "This is hard times. No girl is safe as long as there are hootie macks. It ain't worth it to try to be hip. Just be yourselves, ladies."

"And remember to say your prayers. You know what I'm saying, kids?"

Zu-Zu gave one of the bigger little girls a body bag that she had kept from the talisman and stored in her right shoe, her Achilles' heel trying to understand if bad soles/souls was a black thang. "Keep this," Girl said. "One day you'll need it."

"What makes you think she knows what that is?" I asked Zu-Zu. Zu-Zu put the girl's black hair into a ponytail and rolled a rubber band around it.

She gave me this funky look, like I was low rating her or

something. "Man, if you gotta ask, you'll never know."

The little girl smiled as if she were an African queen doing Shirley Temple, fake jewels in her hair.

"Shoo, scat, go on! Get out of here, you little crumbsnatchers, rug rats, table pimps!" The children moved the crowd. A couple of boys resumed playing with weapons, shooting water at the girls, their guns dripping, the girls tripping, their parents probably at the drugstore too busy sipping liquor to care.

"Not that I care," said Zu-Zu, "but I think we'd better not get involved with any more people's lives. Let's just go. I can take care of us. You know I'm good." Zu-Zu pulled a Chase Visa credit card out of her shoe and flashed it.

"We'd be chased forever, Zu-Zu. You know that. It's all about attitude. Now is the time to stand up for ourselves."

"I ain't going out like Miss Jane Pitman," said Zu-Zu. "If you want to scrap, you'll have to do it by yo'self."

"Cool then. But don't ask me for no favors later."

"You'll never make it without me!" Zu-Zu said, picking at her black fingernail polish.

"Then I'll go to Nigger Heaven trying," I said, "cause I'm cool like dat." I got this digable planet's song in my head.

"We're in a time warp," said Zu-Zu. "There's no time to try to be cute. I got a man. Tell them who I am. Don't play me to the curb. We can find shelter. Let's just do that."

"Go ahead!" I shouted to Zu-Zu. After looking shocked, she spat in my face and took off like a runaway slave.

I searched for an ice cube to help me keep my cool. "Today was a good day," I said to myself. I turned my head only to see Chops put a nigger flicker through my heart. As I fell to the dirt, I heard a distant group of park singers hum "How Do I Say Goodbye to Yesterday." Chops whacked a pear in his hands and showed me the mushy parts. Then he turned me over and stabbed me in the back before running, carrying a slice of apple pie in his mouth and beginning to eat it all up.

I felt my head become dizzy, my big jaws blowing in and out trying to help me breathe. "Doo-wah-diddy," I said angrily, "all this for shit."

For some reason, Chops stopped running and backed up to me while I was rolling around on the ground. He picked up a styrofoam cup filled with dirty liquid and smashed it on his head. He stood there doggin' me out, his fingers digging inside his pants—tucking his shirt in. Chops started telling me that he had to do-do, blaming all of this violence on the system.

Chops was cracking up, but trying to play it off.

"People funny, boy," he said.

I reached for somebody's doo-rag in the grass laying in front of me. Chops stabbed me in the back again.

"Who feels it knows it, Cuz," Chops said. Then he did a ghost, leaving me badly hurt and bleeding, niggas beginning to crowd around and watch me die. A black man in the audience sang "We Are The World" to ease the tension.

I looked at him and smiled. "You wish," I said. But I never knew which way he took it. Zu-Zu came rushing out of nowhere and swep me away again, dragging me several yards through Central Park and begging me to hold on.

"Old niggers never die," Zu-Zu said. "They just dance hoodoo on God's schemes."

I could look into Zu-Zu's eyes and tell that she was struggling to stay strong, and that even she herself wasn't fully convinced of what she had just said. Finally embracing me in her arms, she started singing "Every Goodbye Ain't Gone."

I shut my eyes and once again dreamed of going home, Zu-Zu looking down on me.

I Got The Blues Of A Fallen Teardrop